Ladling with Luke

D.E. BARTLEY

vinci
BOOKS

Vinci Books

vinci-books.com

Published by Vinci Books Ltd in 2026

1

This work is a work of fiction. Names, characters, places and incidents are the product of the author's imagination or are used fictitiously. Any resemblance to actual persons, living or dead, places and incidents is entirely coincidental.

A CIP catalogue record for this book is available from the British Library.

Paperback ISBN: 9781036733858

The EU GPSR authorised representative is Logos Europe, 9 rue Nicolas Poussion, 17000 La Rochelle, France contact@logoseurope.eu

By D.E. Bartley

Lakeside Ranch

Ladling with Luke

Dancing with Dan

O'Reilly Fight Club

Four Stepbrothers & I

Four Daddies & I

Faking it with the SEALs

Three Stepbrothers Save Christmas

Four Fiancés & I

Devil's Playground

Precious Little Rose

The Blood Moon Series

Rogue

Her Protector

To all my readers this holiday season.
Wishing you all a magical, fun and gin filled time.

Chapter One

ELLI

"Hey girl, how did it go?"

I look away from my computer to see Grace standing behind me.

"I'm feeling positive. Hazel seemed pleased with my ideas and Anthony didn't doze off, which is always a good sign. I need to keep my fingers and toes crossed that I win this campaign and promotion" I reply, spinning around in my office chair to face her, holding up my crossed, manicured fingers.

"Girl, with those legs on show and your British accent, it's no wonder Anthony was paying attention." Grace smirks.

I smile as I look down at my grey pencil skirt suit and high heels. That's not why I wore this today, but I'm not going to tell her that.

"Looks like Luke's just come out from doing his pitch. He's looking very smug," Grace says as she looks across to the conference room, her smile quickly disappearing. "Fuck, he's coming over here," she mutters as I moan.

"Howdy, legs!" I hear his solid Southern accent come from behind me. I turn my chair and face Luke with a raised brow.

"I'm sure that's classed as sexual harassment in the workplace, cowboy," I reply, smiling. "Haven't you got anything better to do than spend your day looking at what you'll never get?"

Luke leans on my cubicle wall and looks at me with his sexy, playful grin. It'd be much easier to dislike him if he weren't so damn gorgeous, with his jet-black hair and blue eyes. Don't even get me started on his body.

"I've told you legs," Luke replies with a cheeky wink, "one day you won't be able to fight these desires anymore, and I'm going to show you just how much fun we can have with those long pins wrapped around me." I place my elbows on my desk before leaning my chin on my fists, smiling.

"The only part of you my legs will ever be wrapped around is your neck as I crush your windpipe," I reply. Luke runs his fingers through his hair as he flashes me a mischievous grin.

"I'm telling ya legs, you will succumb to me one day."

"That day will come when you stop being a royal pain in my ass. In other words, never!" I lean back into my chair and cross my arms over my chest.

"Ahh legs, you almost look like you mean it," Luke sighs as he places a hand over his heart and pouts. "Almost!" he adds with a wink before reaching over, picking up my coffee mug, which is half full and strutting off towards his desk on the other side of the floor. "Thanks for the coffee, legs!" he shouts as I flip him off.

"Bloody wanker!" I call after him, trying not to smile.

"I don't know why you don't report him for how he

speaks to you?" Grace says behind me. I turn to face her again as I laugh.

"Nah, he's harmless. He just needs somebody to keep him from getting too big-headed. It's all just friendly banter. Plus, it's fun when I win ad campaigns over him. He sulks for weeks and I get to gloat," I reply with a gleeful grin. "I've got this latest one in the bag; I can feel it."

Grace laughs as she picks up her bag from the floor. "Come on, it's the end of the day and I fancy a few glasses of champagne before we finish tomorrow for Christmas."

"Sounds great; let me grab my stuff, finish this email, and I'll meet you at the entrance," I reply as I turn back to my computer. After all the late nights working on the campaign, I could do with unwinding with a drink or ten.

Luke

"All hail Luke Johnson, the king of advertising. Long may he reign over us lesser peasants, especially those with long legs and British accents." Oliver calls out as he holds up his beer bottle, the other guys from the office all cheer as I shake my head.

"Hey! Only I get to talk about her legs! With me, she knows it's friendly banter; with you it's just perverted."

"Protective of her much, Luke?" Oliver teases, grinning.

"Someone has to watch out for her; she's only been in the States for six months, and that British accent is going to get her into trouble," I argue as I take a sip of my beer.

I'm surprisingly protective of Elli Clarkson. It's not just because she's gorgeous; with her long amber hair, hazel eyes, and curves that make me feel things I haven't felt in years. It's also because she's very quickly become a great friend. With us both having moved to Chicago within the last year, we're still finding our places in work and elsewhere. Plus, the banter is just plain fun.

I feel my phone vibrate in my pocket and quickly pull it out.

Anthony: A fantastic presentation today, Johnson. Be in my office at 9 A.M sharp to discuss how it can be improved so you can move forward with it.

I turn and show the message to Oliver, whose face lights up as he starts cheering.

"I fucking knew you would get it! I never had a single doubt! Time to celebrate, my brother; let's get on the shots!"

Chapter Two

ELLI

I look down at my phone and re-read the message from my boss Anthony for the hundredth time since receiving it last night. My heart's racing with excitement and nerves as I head up in the elevator to the fifteenth floor of the building, where the advertising agency I work for is based. I've worn my favourite trouser suit and my hair down - so it falls in long loose waves down my back - hoping to look as professional as possible.

I quickly head to my desk and dump my bag underneath it before pulling my portfolio from the drawer I locked it in last night. I look down at it and smile, my heart racing. This campaign will be the start of something big for me, I can feel it. It could be the one to push me closer to the life I've been dreaming about since I moved here from the UK six months ago.

It had been one of the scariest moves of my life; I left everything I knew and started afresh. The "starting anew" part wasn't the worst bit, I've done that my whole life. The scariest part of moving across the Atlantic Ocean was that this time I'd invested my life savings in my last ditch attempt to find a place I could finally call home.

I hear my phone vibrate across the desk. I pick it up and look at the screen.

Grace: Go get 'em, girl! Push for that pay rise so we can party in style!

I chuckle as I check the time. Anthony asked me to be at his office at nine, and it's five to now.

I place my phone in the bottom drawer of my desk with my bag and lock it before picking up my folder. I take a deep breath and head toward Anthony's office.

As soon as I get to his door, I knock. I hear him call for me to enter.

I take one last deep breath, open the door, and walk in.

"Sorry, I think I'm a little early," I say as I look at my boss sitting behind his huge mahogany desk with a smile.

"Take a seat, Elli, I'll just finish this call," Anthony replies as he holds his hand out to the two chairs in front of his desk. I take a seat and wait, trying not to listen to the conversation. A few minutes later, Anthony puts down his phone and looks up at me with a smile.

"I'm glad you're a few minutes early as I want to discuss something with you before…" he doesn't get any further as a knock at the door interrupts him. "Ah, I see I won't get to pre-warn you," he chuckles before calling for whoever's knocking to come in.

"Sorry. Am I early?"

I turn to see Luke standing in the doorway; he looks from Anthony to me and frowns.

"No, not at all Luke, please come in and take a seat so we can get started," Anthony says as I watch Luke walk cautiously into the room. I turn around and see our boss looking at us both, smiling.

"I can see you are both a little confused, so let me explain why I've called you both here together," he says as he leans forward in his chair and places his hands together on the desk in front of him.

"I'm going to be frank, as much as we loved both of your presentations yesterday, something was missing from them. I'm not saying they weren't good, but we want to try something new and get you both to work together on this campaign and see if you can come up with something bigger and better," Anthony explains as he looks between us. Luke and I glance at each other.

"You want us to work together?" Luke asks for confirmation. Anthony nods and looks at the two of us individually.

"The chemistry between the two of you has long been a subject of discussions on this floor, and I know you can't deny the fact that when you are competing against each other, you produce your best work. I want to see what will happen when you put that energy into something together," Anthony explains further, before staring at us both as if waiting for us to comment.

I know that Anthony's right; we probably would work superbly together, but a part of me wants to burst into tears. I need this campaign, plus the promotion and pay rise I would get from it. My funds are starting to run low, and living in the States is expensive.

"What about the promotion and bonus? Would it be offered to both of us? Would the money be shared 50/50?" Luke asks next to me. I watch as Anthony nods and slowly smiles, and my heart sinks.

"Yes, but we've asked the company for twice the amount

as they will have two of our best people working for them. They have agreed, so you wouldn't lose out on anything. As for the promotion, it will be offered to both of you," he explains as I let out a breath I didn't realise I was holding.

"What do you both think?" Anthony asks as he looks between us again. I hear Luke sigh next to me, but I still can't bring myself to look at him.

"I'm fine with it if Elli is," I hear him say. I turn to him and see him giving me a soft, reassuring smile. "Do you think you can handle working with me? Or would you end up pushing me out the window like you keep threatening to?" he asks with that lop-sided smile that puts me at ease. I nod before turning back to Anthony, hoping I can hide how fast my heart is racing.

"Okay," I answer as I force my shoulders to relax. "How long do we have to get this together?"

Chapter Three

LUKE

"Two weeks? He's giving you two weeks to work out a new campaign with Hermione Granger, of all people? How the hell are you going to do that? Aren't you going home tomorrow?" Oliver curses in the coffee room as I try and get my head around everything.

This morning hasn't gone as I thought it would. I never in a million years dreamt that I'd be sharing this campaign with anyone, let alone Elli.

"I bet this is all her doing. She didn't win the campaign outright, so she asked to be paired up with you," Oliver goes on; I look up at him from my spot on the staff couch and frown.

"Elli was as blindsided as I was. She was still in a state of shock when we left his office."

"Or she's just a good actor," Oliver mutters.

"Enough, Oliver; she had no idea or input with this, and I've told you before about calling her names!" I snap as I get to my feet and head back to the coffee machine.

Why the hell did I drink so much last night? My head's

pounding, and I want to go back to my apartment and sleep it off.

"Mom will have kittens when I tell her I can't go home. She was sulking enough over me missing Thanksgiving; to miss Christmas as well will devastate her." I sigh as I pour my coffee and wonder how I'll tell her. Mom's struggled with my decision to leave Alabama and move to Chicago for work. She's used to family sticking close. But I needed to get away and try a different life, even if that meant breaking her heart.

"Luke?" I turn to find Elli standing in the doorway of the staffroom.

I'd watched the colour drain from her face this morning as Anthony told us we would be working together. At first, I thought it might have been because of the reduced money, so I asked how much we'd be getting, but then I realised it might be me. Maybe I've pushed the banter too far and offended her?

"Hey, what's up?" I ask as I take a sip of my coffee.

"I've booked the conference room for the day so we can devise a plan," she says as she glares at Oliver, who is staring at her. These two have never gotten along for some reason.

"Cool, I'll grab my stuff and meet you in there. Want a coffee?" I ask as I turn to pick up her mug from the side.

"That'd be great, thanks, and don't drink it; I haven't had one yet!" Elli warns before turning around and heading out the door.

"I'm going to go and research English villains, so I have more creative names to call the witch," Oliver groans as he heads over to me and the coffee machine. I quickly slap him around the back of the head. "Hey man, what the hell was that for?" he protests, rubbing his head.

"If I hear you have been giving her shit, you'll have me

to deal with," I growl in warning as I make her coffee and leave the room before Oliver can say anything else that's likely to piss me off.

I walk to my desk and place the two coffees down before sitting in my chair and turning my laptop on to check that I have everything I think we'll need. My desk phone starts ringing, and I quickly pick it up.

"Luke Johnson," I answer as I hold the receiver between my shoulder and head.

"You bought my Christmas present yet?" a chirpy voice calls through the phone. I sigh as I roll my eyes.

"Why? What have you seen now, Lily?" I ask, knowing she'll want me to pick her up some designer bag or purse. She's been asking for various gifts since August.

"Well, you know I'm your favourite baby sister?"

"You're my only baby sister, but go on," I cut in, chuckling as I flick through a few emails on my screen.

"Still your favourite, and I just saw a gorgeous Ralph Lauren purse, and I was wondering if you wanted to buy it for me?" she asks in that sweet voice she gets when she wants something.

"Send me the link, and I'll see what I can do," I sigh as I realise I won't have time to post the gifts to ensure they arrive by Christmas.

"What's up with you?" Lily asks. I should have known she'd pick up on my mood.

"I can't make it back for the holidays," I admit as I lean back into my chair and run my fingers through my hair.

"What! Why?" she gasps.

"Somethings come up in work," I explain. Hating that it sounds like an excuse.

"But it's the holidays! Shouldn't the place be closed?" she asks, outraged.

"It's not as simple as that, Lils," I sigh.

"Luke, Mom's going to flip. She's been talking non-stop about you coming home for weeks!"

"I know, it's going to break her heart. It's not like I'm happy about it, Lils. But it's work; what am I meant to do?" I ask.

"You're meant to come home for a week; surely that's not too much?" Lily snaps. If she's taking the news this badly, I dread telling Mom.

I see Elli walking into the conference room and sigh.

"Look, I have to go, don't tell Mom yet; I'll phone her when I know more. Maybe I can manage a couple of days at least," I sigh as I rub the back of my neck.

"All right, but make sure you tell her soon," Lily demands.

"I will," I reply as Lily says bye and hangs up. I let out a deep breath and close my laptop, quickly sliding it into my shoulder bag along with my portfolio. I sling it over my head and grab the two coffees before heading into the conference room.

I walk in, and as I expected, Elli has already set up notebooks, her laptop, and different colour pens on the table as she wipes down two whiteboards; she is always so organised. I can't stop myself from admiring her as she stands with her back to me. She's wearing a pantsuit, making her curves look even more perfect. Her fitted top hugs that waist perfectly, and her hair hangs down her back in waves stopping just as her back dips before that perfectly round ass comes into view. No matter what she wears, her curves do things to me that no woman has ever managed before. And don't get me started on those long pins. I remember the first time I saw her; it was like they went on forever; hence the nickname, legs. Not that I'd let anyone else call her it; it's between the two of us only.

"Are you going to come in, cowboy? Or are you just going to stand there staring at what you'll never have?" Elli asks without turning to face me.

"Who said I was staring at you? Maybe the sight of all this stationery is what's stopping me in my tracks?" I reply, grinning. Elli turns around and looks at me with an arched brow as she places a hand on her curvy hip. I quickly wink, causing her to roll her eyes; although I still manage to catch a glimpse of the smile she attempts to hide from me.

"Did you leave anything in the supply closet for anyone else?" I ask as I walk to a seat at the top of the table and look down at everything set out on it in perfect order. I reach out for a pad of sticky notes, but Elli slaps my hand.

"Ouch, legs! Don't worry; I wasn't going to steal them," I chuckle as I push her mug towards her and take a seat with my own.

I watch as Elli lifts her mug to her lips, closes her eyes and lets that first sip wash down her throat as if it's touching her soul. I've noticed she does this whenever she's feeling under pressure. Elli's coffee calms her like an alcoholic's first drink of the day calms their addiction. I leave her to clear her mind and relax a little. I once interrupted her as she drank her first cup of coffee of the day; that was the first time she threatened to throw me out of a window. I've learnt from my mistakes and only ever push her when I know she's caffeinated.

Elli looks at me as she takes a seat.

"I heard you on the phone. I know you're meant to be going home for Christmas; you should go," she says as she leans back in her chair. I copy her as I grin playfully.

"So you can do all the work, take most of the credit and

get the promotion alone?" I ask, joking. Elli shakes her head and looks into her cup as she answers.

"You have family looking forward to seeing you. Spend time with them whilst you can. It's Christmas, after all, a time for family and friends," she says before taking another sip of her drink. "We can communicate through email and video chat," she adds; before a smile creeps onto her lips. "I'm sure even cowboys have internet access," she teases.

"I'll think about it. What are your plans for the holidays? You not going back to the UK to see family?" I ask. I can't miss the sad look that flashes across her eyes before she tries to hide it.

"No, it's not as easy for me to go back and forth," she whispers before taking another sip of coffee as I frown at her.

"What will you be doing? Spending Christmas alone?"

Elli shrugs and looks around us, obviously trying to avoid eye contact, but our eyes meet for a few seconds, and I can't miss their sadness. The words leave my mouth before I stop to think, "Come back with me."

"What?" Elli asks, her eyes popping open. Shit, why did I say that? She couldn't come back with me, could she? But then the thought of her being on her own over Christmas seems wrong.

"Come to Alabama with me. We can work on the campaign, and you won't be alone for Christmas," I reply, desperately trying to decide whether this is a good idea.

"I can't go back with you! What would your family think?" she argues as she sits up.

"Nothing; they'd be happy to have you there," I answer with a shrug.

"But it's Christmas! They won't want a stranger with

them. Thanks for the offer, Luke, but no," she answers, shaking her head.

"Would you come if it wasn't Christmas? Is that the problem? I won't let you spend the holidays on your own, legs." I sit up and look across the table at her, "When was the last time you took a break from this place? I know you were here right through Thanksgiving; I didn't say anything as you're British and don't celebrate it. But I *know* you celebrate Christmas, so come with me and have the break you need. I'll take you around and show you the sights during the day, and we can work in the evenings. What do you say?" I ask, suddenly feeling excited about the prospect of being able to show her my home town and introduce her to my family. I can see Elli's thinking about it, but then she shakes her head again.

"I can't put your family out like that. It's not fair." She stands up and walks over to the whiteboard as if to end the conversation, but I'm far from finished. I pull out my phone and quickly connect a call.

"Howdy, Pops," I say as soon as my dad answers. Elli spins around and stares at me open-mouthed, but I ignore her. "Can you put Mom on? I need to ask her something," I hear my mom coming to the phone.

"Lily says you're not coming home," Mom says as soon as she has the phone. I should have known Lily would never keep her mouth shut.

"No, I am, but mind if I bring someone with me? They ain't from round here, and I don't want her spending the holidays alone."

"A girl? It's Elli, isn't it?" Mom asks. Have I spoken about her to Mom?

"Yeah, it is," I reply as Elli waves her hands at me and mouths "no" dramatically, but I wink at her, smiling.

"Of course, she's welcome; no one should be alone at Christmas," Mom says excitedly.

"Thanks, Mom. I'll call you later with details," I reply as I hang up and look at Elli, smirking.

"I can't believe you just did that, you absolute tosser!" she growls.

"Now you have to come. Otherwise, Mom will be heartbroken, and you can't do that to the old dear," I say with a grin.

"You're impossible, do you know that?" Elli snaps as she runs her fingers through her hair, looking a little stressed.

"Yep. So what do you say, legs? You gonna spend the holidays with me?"

Elli looks at me and sighs, her shoulders slumping in defeat.

"Fine! What's the weather like in Alabama this time of year?"

Chapter Four

ELLI

What the hell was I thinking agreeing to spend the week with Luke and his family? What if they hate me and spend the week forcibly being nice to me? Or worse, what if they hate me and show it? Oh God, what have I done?

I look out the window of the truck Luke's brother had left at the airport for us and try to distract myself from the growing worry tightening in my stomach. It works as the view is gorgeous; I'll give him that. Why would you move away from this to live in Chicago? Then again, this is Luke we're talking about; he never seems to do the expected.

"So, umm, there's something I should warn you about before we get there." I turn away from the window and look at Luke as he drives with one hand on the wheel, and one arm leaning out of the open window. He looks more relaxed than I've ever seen him before.

"Go on," I reply suspiciously.

"So, you heard the conversation with my mom? Well, it seems she thinks we're dating, and I haven't had the heart to tell her we aren't."

"WHAT? Please tell me you're joking!" I cry as I turn to face him. Luke cringes, and I realise he's not. "Well, you need to put her straight when we get there!" I demand. Luke looks at me, and I know he's about to argue.

"The thing is she's excited about me having a girlfriend, as I don't date, and I think she thought all hope was lost on me," Luke explains, chancing a glance at me.

I stare at him, confused. "You, Luke Johnson, don't date? I thought you were the stud cowboy who never went to an event without a date?" I cross my arms over my chest, not believing him in the slightest!

"Most of the time, they're just friends. Once or twice, I've taken Oliver's sister as she's trying to get into modelling and uses the events to get the interaction she needs," he admits, refusing to look back at me.

"Oliver's sister? Are you serious right now?" I laugh. Luke frowns at me.

"What? I'm just helping her out. We've never … you know," he says as he raises his brows.

"You've never had sex with her. Is that what you mean? You can say the word, cowboy," I laugh whilst shaking my head.

"Yeah, well, anyway," he says, changing the subject. I look at him and realise his cheeks are flushed from embarrassment. It's a cute look on him, not one I often see.

"I'm not pretending to be your girlfriend," I repeat, shaking my head to prove a point.

"Oh, come on, you won't have to do anything. Let me wrap my arm around you now and again or kiss you on the cheek. That's no more than I do with you anyway," Luke protests.

"Yeah, but…" I try to find an argument, but I can't. Luke and I can be very flirty, but it's usually when we are winding each other up and part of the gloating when we get a contract over the other. A plan quickly pops into my head.

"Fine, I'll play along, but I have conditions," I answer as I turn to look at him again.

"Go on," he says cautiously.

"As we have to produce this campaign together, I want my name to go first so that I'm the lead consultant with the company," I state. Luke looks at me and frowns.

"What if I say no?" he asks.

"Then I won't play along, and I will tell your mum the truth," I reply with a grin. I watch Luke as he looks at the road and thinks about it.

"Fine," he replies through gritted teeth, before glancing at me. "Your name goes first, and you're the lead consultant."

I hold my hand out, which he quickly takes, and we shake.

"That's a good boy. It's a pleasure doing business with you," I tease before going back to looking out the window, but my smile quickly dissolves.

"Hang on, what will the sleeping arrangements be?" I demand.

"What? Don't trust yourself to share a bed with me, legs? Scared you'll finally give in to those sexual urges?" Luke glances at me with a wide, devious but sexy grin.

"Not happening. You'd better have religious parents that don't allow bed-sharing before marriage," I declare. Luke laughs shaking his head.

"No, they'll allow us to share a bed, and we'll sleep in my room." I quickly open my mouth to protest, but Luke cuts me off. "Don't worry; there's a couch in there; I'll sleep on that. No one will know. It's not like they will risk barging in."

I tighten my lips and go back to looking out the windscreen.

"That's better than sharing a bed, I guess." I hear Luke chuckling next to me, but I don't bother turning to look at him. I'm too mesmerised by the giant metal archway in the distance.

I've heard about ranches and seen pictures, but I've never seen one in real life. That must be the entrance to one. My breath catches in my throat when Luke turns off and drives under the arch and down the road.

"You live on a ranch?" I ask amazed as Luke nods, frowning.

"Don't tell me you didn't know?" he chuckles.

"I wouldn't be asking if I did, would I? You're a real-life cowboy!" I add, making Luke laugh aloud.

"I thought that was why you call me it," he says as I shake my head.

"I call you it because of your accent. I had no idea you were one!" I point out, unable to keep the shock from my voice.

"Well, looks like you're about to learn a lot of other stuff about me, legs," Luke states as he smiles, "you never know, I may learn a little more about you too."

"Or not!" I go back to looking out the window, even more eagerly than before.

Chapter Five

LUKE

My heart's racing as I pull to a stop outside the main house. I look over at Elli and see the wonder in her eyes. I never dreamt she would look this excited about the old ranch. It's been in my family since my great-grandfather built it over one hundred and fifty years ago. Over time the land we own has expanded, as well as the number of livestock and crops with it.

When you compare it to the modern lights and sounds of Chicago, it isn't much to look at, but I hope Elli doesn't hate her time here. It felt like a good idea to bring her so we could get the campaign done and she could take the well-deserved break she needed. Elli thinks no one's noticed how tired she looks now and again or how miserable she is at times, but I have, and I want to be able to give her a way to recharge and unwind. It was one of the reasons I asked her to come along with me. But I still worry I've made a grave mistake and that she might not be as relaxed or happy here as I'd hoped.

I climb out of the pickup and head over to open Elli's door, but she's already out and looking around.

"It's not much, but it's home," I say as I approach her. Elli spins around and stares at me, her eyes bright and full.

"Not much? It's a freaking ranch! It's amazing!" she squeals excitedly, almost hopping on the spot. I can't help but chuckle at her excitement, instantly relaxing.

"Come on then, I'll give you a tour of the main house," I chuckle as I hold out my hand for her; she looks at it for a second and surprises me when she takes it with the smallest eye roll. "The tour of the land will have to wait for another time as we're losing light," I explain as I pull her towards me and start heading to the house hand in hand. We don't get more than a few steps when the front door opens, and I see my niece.

"Uncle Luke," she squeals as she rushes towards us with her arms out, her long dark brown hair flowing behind her. I let go of Elli's hand and squat down, my arms out wipe. My niece jumps into them eagerly and wraps her arms around my neck, squeezing me tightly.

"Howdy, sweetheart," I laugh as I hug her back. I turn to Elli and find her smiling at us. "I would like you to meet someone," I whisper to my niece as she pulls away from me slightly. I balance her on my hip and turn us.

"Elli, this is my niece Skyla. Skyla, this is my friend, Elli." Elli steps forward and looks at Skyla with a soft smile on her face.

"Hello, Skyla; it's nice to meet you," she says softly. Skyla looks at her for a moment and then smiles at me.

"She's pretty," she says before turning back to Elli.

"That she is," I reply without hesitation. Elli looks away, but I can't miss the embarrassed smile on her face or the way her cheeks become flushed.

"Skyla Johnson, I told you to wait in the house."

We all turn to see my sister-in-law standing on the front porch—her hands on her hips and a smile on her face. I lower Skyla down to the ground, and she surprises me by walking straight to Elli and taking her hand before tugging it. Elli smiles as she squats down and lets Skyla whisper in her ear.

"I was meant to let Uncle Luke bring you to the house, but I couldn't wait." Elli looks from Skyla to me and smiles.

"Well, how about you take us both, and we will stick up for you," Elli whispers back. Skyla smiles and moves between us before taking our hands and pulling us towards the house where her mother is standing, smiling.

"What can I say? She was happy to see me," I say with a smile as we climb to the front porch. I lean in and kiss her on the cheek before turning to Elli. "Elli, this is my sister-in-law, Rachel," I introduce them quickly; both women look at each other with wide grins.

"Well, Hi! It's nice to finally put a face to the name," Rachel chirps as she and Elli shake hands.

"Thanks, it's lovely to meet you," she replies smiling.

If I didn't know Elli as I do, I'd miss the nervous way she's rubbing her fingers together as soon as Skyla rushes to her mom. Elli always does this while waiting to do a presentation at work. I step closer and entwine my fingers into hers, hoping to calm her. Skyla's being scolded by her mother for not listening, so neither of them hears me as I whisper to Elli.

"Don't be nervous. I promise they don't bite."

Elli looks down at our hands. I'm about to let go, worried I'm making matters worse when I feel her fingers tighten around mine. I look into her hazel eyes as she gives me a soft smile. I spot Skyla and her mom disappearing into the house; Rachel gives me a wink as they go. Elli looks at me, and I can't miss how nervous she suddenly is.

"I've never done the whole 'meet the parents' thing before.... even with real relationships," she admits in a whisper. I smile at her and squeeze her hand gently.

"Me neither, so it's a first for the both of us," I answer winking, which earns me a chuckle. "Come on. I promise you they'll be on their best behaviour," I reassure her as I lead her into the house, not missing the deep breath she takes before entering.

Chapter Six

ELLI

Luke leads me into the house through the entrance hall and a large dining room with a vast wooden table set with nine places. I keep hold of his hand as his touch calms my racing heart and stops me from turning on my heels and running for the door. The old anxiety which comes with meeting new people causes my hands to shake. Luke must realise as he tightens his grip momentarily before letting go and placing a reassuring arm around my waist, tugging me against his side.

"They're going to love you; stop worrying," he whispers in my ear as he leads me passed the table and towards a doorway at the back of the room, where I can hear several people whispering, especially that one little voice that sounds above the rest.

"She's beautiful!" Skyla giggles, quickly followed by the sound of her mother hushing her.

"See, you made a good impression already," Luke chuckles next to me. As we near the door, I find my step faltering, but Luke's there with a soft push as he moves his arm from around me and places his hand on the bottom of my back.

"Breathe, legs," he whispers before moving his hand from my back and retaking mine like he knows exactly what I need.

As soon as we walk through the doorway, five heads turn to look at us.

"Well, look what the cat dragged in. The big city boy's finally come home," a tall guy beside Rachel calls grinning.

"Billy Johnson, you leave your bother alone," a woman with short salt and pepper hair says as she walks up behind Billy and slaps him around the back of the head, just like I have seen Luke do to Oliver so many times; I can't help but chuckle at the similarity. "And don't be trying to embarrass him in front of Elli either," she adds as she walks up to the two of us. I feel Luke let go of my hand as he steps forward and pulls her into a hug.

"Howdy, Mom," I hear him say as he kisses her cheek.

"Glad you finally found your way back home," she chuckles before stepping back from her son and walking towards me. Before I know what's happening, she pulls me into a hug and squeezes. I chuckle as I hug her back. She steps back but holds me at arm's length.

"And so glad we finally get to meet you, Elli," she says, smiling.

"It's lovely to meet you too. Thank you so much for having me, Mrs Johnson," I reply.

"There's no need to thank us, we're just so glad you could come. And please, call me Annie," she says before looking back at her son, who is now hugging whom I can only guess is his father. Luke turns and looks at me, smiling as he stands back beside me.

"Elli, this is my Pops, William," he says as he holds his

hand towards his dad, who is an older version of Luke. His dad walks towards me with his hand out, which I take and shake.

"It's good to finally meet you, Elli. I like hearing how you keep this one on his toes at work. I hope you're keeping that head of his in check."

I smile at his dad as I relax further. "Oh, I certainly do. That's why I only let him win a campaign if I'm too busy myself," I chuckle.

"Hey, I won that last one fair and square," Luke protests beside me. I turn and look at him with a raised eyebrow.

"Your only competition for that one was Oliver because I was too busy," I point out.

"Still won it, legs," Luke replies with a grin. I roll my eyes as I shake my head.

"Whatever, cowboy," I sigh, not missing the wink he gives me. I hear a deep laugh coming from the other side of the room. I turn to see Billy walking up to me. He pulls me into what can only be described as a bear hug as he lifts me off my feet.

"Hey! Be careful with her, Billy," I hear Annie call next to me, but I laugh as he places my feet back on the floor.

"I'm fine, I promise," I chuckle as Billy and Luke hug whilst slapping each other on the back.

"Glad to see she's keeping you in line, little brother. It's about time someone made an honest man out of you," Billy laughs slapping Luke on the back again. I always thought Luke was well-built, but looking at him next to Billy, he's quite a bit smaller. Billy is built more like a bear, whereas Luke is defined and his muscle mass more toned.

"Yeah, thanks, man," Luke sighs before stepping back from his brother. Suddenly a scream comes from behind us, and Luke only turns in time to catch the young woman who throws herself at him.

"You're finally here!" she screams so loud I see Luke quickly move his head away from her as if to protect his ear.

"Hey to you too, Lils," he laughs as he hugs her before she jumps out of his arms and turns to me with a massive smile.

"Oh my god, you came!" she squeals before pulling me into a tight hug. I laugh as I look over her shoulder at Luke, who mouths "sorry" at me; I chuckle and hug her back.

"Lily, will you let the poor girl breathe already!" Luke sighs as he pulls her off me. Lily turns around and sticks her tongue out at him. "This little whirlwind is my sister, Lily," Luke laughs as he throws his arm around her shoulder. I notice him looking around, "where's Grams?" he asks, frowning.

"She went for a nap but will join us at dinner," Annie says, smiling at her son. "Rachel, can you go and wake her, please? She'll need at least half an hour to wake up properly," Annie adds with a smile as she threads her arm through Lily's and pulls her from Luke's side.

"Luke, why don't you show Elli where your room is? I'm sure you both want to freshen up before dinner after travelling most of the day."

"Freshening up sounds perfect," I sigh at the thought of a shower or at least a wash.

"I'll go and grab the bags from the truck," Luke says as he smiles at me.

"I'll give you a hand," I reply quickly as I walk up to him.

"What's up, legs? Don't trust me with your bags?" Luke laughs as he places a hand on the bottom of my back and follows me through the doorway.

"You dropped your bag twice. Are you surprised I don't want to risk you carrying mine?" I ask as we head back through the dining room.

"I was distracted; it wasn't my fault," he protests as he catches up with me, and we head out the front door to the truck.

"Distracted by the bridal party that was waiting for our flight?" I ask with an arched brow. Luke turns to face me, grinning.

"When I had you in those tight jeans next to me? They didn't compare to you, legs," he replies with a wink before walking outside as I feel my stomach flutter from the compliment.

It's pitch black outside now, and I can only see thanks to the bright porch light. I follow Luke down to the truck, and he opens the cover on the back.

"I'm sorry about that lot; I never realised how excited they would be. I'll tell them the truth if it's too much," Luke says quietly as he looks down into the truck bed as if trying to avoid eye contact. I walk up to him and lean against the drivers' side door.

"It's fine. I don't want to cause any tension over Christmas. I guess it's not that bad pretending to be your girlfriend for a week," I reply, smiling softly. Luke looks at me with arched brows.

"No?"

I smile as I shake my head.

"No, it could be worse," I point out. Luke turns to face me as he leans against the truck with his arms crossed over his broad chest.

"Oh really? And how's that, legs?" He asks, grinning.

"You could be Oliver," I reply, winking. Luke throws his

head back and laughs before throwing his arm around my shoulders and pulling me against him in a hug.

"Thanks, legs. You're one of a kind," he whispers as he plants a kiss on the top of my head. I can't stop myself from hugging him back.

It'll be easy acting like I have feelings for Luke; I just have to hope it will be as easy to walk away once this week is over.

Chapter Seven

LUKE

I'm lying on the couch in my room, staring at the ceiling with my hands behind my head, wondering how I made it through dinner without anyone realising something was wrong.

Everything had been going fine, perfect, in fact. My family instantly fell in love with Elli, as I knew they would. Everyone was laughing and joking until Pops opened his mouth.

"So, Elli, what did your parents think of you moving to the States," he asked as he bit into his dinner roll. I sensed Elli stiffen next to me, and I turned my full attention to her as I realised I had never asked her about her family back in England.

"Oh. Umm, they've passed away," Elli responded nervously next to me. I felt my stomach drop as I had no idea.

"Oh, bless your heart; I'm sorry to hear that. I hope William hasn't upset you by bringing it up," my mom said as she gave her husband the side eye. But Elli just chuckled and shook her head.

"Honestly, it's fine. It was a very long time ago. He hasn't upset me at all," Ellis says reassuringly.

"So, who brought you up?" Pops asked as Mom and I snapped at him to stop. But Elli chuckled nervously.

"Honestly, it's fine. My dad's mum brought me up until I was twelve, but then she passed, and I went into care until I was eighteen. My life led me to where I am now, so I can't resent it or regret anything," she smiled, looking at me before returning to her food.

It was left at that, and people quickly changed the subject to her work and if she liked the States. But the whole time, I couldn't shake the feeling of guilt for not knowing about her past. We're friends; why had I never asked about her family? No wonder she was so adamant that I came home for the holidays. She knows how important it is to spend time with family and how they aren't around forever.

The door from my en-suite opens, and Elli walks out wearing tight shorts and a t-shirt as she ties her hair up before falling onto the bed with a groan.

"I'm so freaking tired," she moans as she starfishes the bed sideways. I give a half-hearted chuckle in response, which causes her to raise her head.

"What's up with you?" she asks, frowning.

"Nothing. Why?" I answer a little eagerly.

"You've been acting strange since dinner. Did I say something wrong?" she asks as she grabs a pillow and moves, so her head is at the bottom of the bed. She lies on her stomach, looking at me, hugging the pillow.

"You haven't upset me, legs," I say with a small smile.

"Then something's got to you, and I'm going to keep

bugging you until you tell me," she says with a cheeky grin that makes my smile more genuine.

"If you must know, I feel bad because I had no idea about your family. I thought we were friends, yet I know nothing about you," I admit. Elli bites her bottom lip before taking a deep breath.

"I'll be honest; part of what I said was a lie. It's easier than telling the truth to people I just met," Elli says, looking towards the door as if wondering if anyone can hear her.

"Which part?" I ask carefully.

"My mum's not dead; well, I don't think she is," she says as she looks at me, and I can see the worry in her eyes.

"Then why say it?" I ask, wondering how she could lie about something like that.

"Because it's easier. It's better than saying she never wanted me. You're the first person I have admitted the truth to in many years," Elli says before taking a deep breath. "She left when I was two months old and never came back. Social services reached out to her when Dad died and again when Nan passed away, but she told them to put me into care. She never wanted kids, and my dad made her keep me. As soon as she had the chance to run, she did."

I watch as Elli blinks a few times and then rolls onto her back and looks up to the ceiling. She puts both arms over her face. "Are you mad at me for lying?" I hear her ask quietly. I stand up and sit on the bed next to her. I take her arms and pull them away from her face.

"Look at me, legs," I whisper. Elli takes another deep breath and looks at me. "I could never be mad at you for telling me the truth. I'm sorry you went through that, but thank you for trusting me," I say softly as I look into her tear-filled eyes.

"You are easy to trust," Elli says quietly. I take her hand

and lift it to my mouth before kissing her knuckles, feeling honoured that she would open up to me. "Well, now you know as much about me as I do you," Elli says, smiling at me, obviously trying to lighten the mood.

"You don't know that much about me," I scoff as I look at her. Elli raises her eyebrows and sits up, so she's sitting cross-legged on the bed in front of me.

"Your favourite colour is green; you hate wearing a shirt and tie but for some reason insist on it. If you could drive any car, it would be a truck. And as much as you tolerate Oliver, you hate that he's a player. Also, you would love to go to Hawaii," she says, counting each one on a finger. I stare at her, amazed.

"How do you know all that?" I ask, frowning at her as she smiles back at me.

"I'm very observant. Every one of your presentations has some element of green in it, that's why I suggested the green background for ours. Whenever you are at work, you constantly fuss with your tie and shirt collar like they are strangling you. I've also seen you drive in the city, and today you looked more comfortable in that truck than you ever do in a car. Plus, we've all heard you snapping at Oliver when he goes on about his 'conquests', and Hawaii was a guess after I saw how excited you were with the possibility of this campaign taking us there," she states with a shrug.

"And I didn't even know about your past," I whisper. "I'm sorry I didn't ask you about it before. At least if I had known, I could have saved you that heartache tonight," I add, looking down at the bed covers underneath us. Elli reaches over and takes my hand, and squeezes it gently.

"You have asked me about my family, but I changed the subject. I didn't want you to feel as sorry for me as you do now," she says, giving me that soft smile.

"Well, I should have tried harder," I reply.

"Why?" she asks, frowning.

"Because I want to know all about you. I want to know *your* favourite colours and where *you* want to travel to. I want to know everything there is to know about you," I admit. Elli moves over and lies down before patting the space next to her on the bed.

"Then lie down and ask me anything, and I'll answer honestly," she whispers.

I face her as we both lie on our sides and start telling each other everything there is to know about ourselves. We lie there on the bed talking for what feels like hours until she falls asleep mid-sentence. I grab a blanket and pull it over us as I lean over to kiss her forehead before returning to lying on my side and watching her sleep as I drift off with a smile.

Chapter Eight

ELLI

I wake up alone, still at the bottom of the bed. At some point in the night, I pulled the duvet over me, or did Luke do it? Did he sleep on the bed with me? Or did he move back to the sofa?

I'm surprised by how much we talked about last night. It was so easy opening up to him about everything. Then again, I've always found it easy to talk to him; even the first day we met, we clicked. Maybe that's just the kind of guy he is.

I stretch and realise that not only has Luke gone, but the sofa shows no signs of someone sleeping on it. Would it be that bad if we shared a bed every night? It's not like anything would happen between us. I shake my head as I let down my hair, climb out of bed, and reach for my phone. I look at the screen and realise it's after ten. I never sleep in this late. What are his family going to think of me? I quickly wash and throw some clothes on before heading downstairs, not knowing where I should go or where Luke is. Has he been up long?

I head into the kitchen in the hope of finding some coffee before I go into withdrawal. Because that's the last thing I want Luke's family to see; they will wonder what the hell their son is dating. Not that we are dating, of course.

I walk into the kitchen to find Annie and Rachel helping Skyla cut out sugar cookies.

"Morning Elli, take it you slept well?" Annie asks with a smile.

"Yeah, sorry. I can't remember the last time I slept in this late," I admit rubbing the back of my neck nervously.

"Don't apologise; Luke's been saying how hard you work for a while. It's not surprising you slept in. It's probably helped how quiet it is out here," Annie says as she wipes her hands on her apron.

"Does Luke talk about me often?" I ask, confused. Rachel and Annie share a look and smile.

"Just about every phone call home," Rachel answers, grinning at me. I feel my cheeks heat as I look away, smiling, unable to ignore the butterflies that start flapping in my stomach. Why does that make me so happy?

"Luke's not long popped in and made a pot of coffee, warning us all to make sure there was some left for you when you woke up," Annie says with a wink. I can't help smiling.

"He learnt his lesson the first time he tried to talk to me before my first cup of coffee at work; it wasn't pretty," I chuckle as I look around. "Where is Luke?" I ask as Annie walks over, smiling, handing me a mug of coffee.

"He's been out helping William and Billy since five. He should be back soon. Do you want sugar or cream?" she asks.

"Just black is fine by me," I reply as I take my first sip. I look at Skyla and her mom.

"Someone's been busy this morning. I love sugar biscuits," I say as Skyla looks at me and frowns.

"They're not biscuits, silly. They're cookies," she declares.

"Sorry, I forget the differences between the English and American names for things," I chuckle as Skyla shakes her head at me like I'm the silliest woman she has ever met.

"We are making *cookies* for Santa and his elves," Skyla says as her face lights up.

"He's going to love them. In England, we leave him mince pies," I explain. This time, everyone turns and frowns at me.

"Santa doesn't eat meat pies!" Skyla yells in disgust. I burst out laughing; just as Luke walks into the kitchen in a pair of jeans, and a tight white t-shirt, which is wet with sweat. His flannel shirt is chucked over his shoulder. I can't help but stare as his muscles show through the fabric. He walks over to me, picks up my mug before finishing what's left of my coffee, and throws in a wink for good measure. I quickly realise I'm still staring and look away.

"What's this about meat pies?" he asks as he leans over and plants a kiss on my head, as he whispers in my ear, "like what you see, legs?" I quickly push him away, shaking my head at him, unable to hide the smile on my face as he laughs out loud.

"Not that kind of mince pie," I answer before turning my attention back to Skyla, trying to ignore the smirks on Annie and Rachel's faces. "It's a mixture of apples, raisins, currants and other bits. It's very yummy, I promise," I chuckle. "It was always my favourite part of Christmas, helping my Nanny make the mince pies," I admit for the first time out loud in many years.

"Will you make some for us so we can try them?" Annie

asks softly. I look up at her and nod, smiling. Excited to be making my Nanny's old favourites again.

"Of course, I think I still remember her recipe. I may need to get a few bits." I answer.

"Let me get changed, and I'll take you. I'm fixin' to go to the store for Pops anyway as he wants me to do a few jobs Billy can't," Luke calls as he refills my mug and takes a sip before handing it to me. I look down at my half-full mug.

"Am I ever going to get a full mug to myself again?" I call after him as he walks out of the kitchen. His ass looks great in his jeans, much better than in his work trousers.

"Nope!" he calls back, laughing. I open my mouth to call out an insult but quickly close it when I remember the five-year-old in the room.

"You two are too cute," Rachel says, smirking at me. Although I hardly hear her as I'm busy watching Luke walk away.

Chapter Nine

LUKE

I've had the best day with Elli. After catching her checking me out this morning, we've flirted constantly. Whilst out in town picking up supplies, we held hands; or I would have my arm around her shoulders or her waist. It's becoming hard to keep my hands to myself. If I'm honest, the more time I spend with her *pretending* that we're in a relationship, it's evident that we *should* be in one.

As soon as we got back from town, I returned to one of the barns and start making the repairs Pops needs. I was worried Elli was going to be fed up as I had promised her that if she came to Alabama, I would show her the sights during the day, but every time I mentioned it, she seemed more than happy to stay at the house with Mom. I've popped in a few times, and the two of them have been deep in conversation. If it's not my mom she's laughing with, it's Rachel and Lily. Elli has fit into the family straight away, and it seems to make her happier than I've ever seen her.

It's coming to five in the evening, and I'm finally finished doing most of the little jobs needed. I walk through the back door and into the kitchen, where Elli is singing quietly to herself whilst peeling the potatoes for dinner. She looks stunning in her tight jeans and a fitted t-shirt. She has a red flannel over the top, buttoned up to her chest, where her breasts bulge. Her hair is tied half up, and the rest hangs down her back. As she sings, she moves her hips causing her round ass to sway. I can't help leaning against the wall, with my arms crossed over my chest, as I watch her with a smile on my face.

Elli is so lost in her own little world that she jumps when she turns around and spots me.

"Christ cowboy, you scared the crap out of me!" she cries as she places her hand on her chest. I chuckle as I walk up to her and wrap my arms around her shoulders, pulling her in for a hug.

"Sorry, legs," I chuckle as I kiss the top of her head and feel her arms go around my waist.

"You smell like sawdust and sweat," Elli laughs as I step back from her.

"I'm sorry. We can't all smell like freshly baked bread," I reply with a smile. Elli grins up at me.

"I never said it was a bad smell!" she chuckles as she playfully pushes against my chest. "Your mum taught me to make dinner rolls," she declares proudly. She walks to the other counter and holds up a basket of rolls. "See, I made these." I walk over and pick one up and feel it's still warm. I squeeze it and take a bite.

"This tastes amazing, legs," I say with a mouth full of bread. Elli blushes as she puts the basket back down.

"I was thinking, how about I take you to one of my favourite places to relax with a beer after dinner? I'll light a fire so we don't get too cold, and hopefully, it will be a clear night, so we will be able to see the stars," I offer as I look into Elli's bright eyes.

"That sounds amazing," Elli says excitedly.

"Leave it with me then. Just make sure you have a warm coat and hat." I call with a smile as I turn around and head out of the kitchen.

As I walk up the stairs, I see Mom putting some stuff away.

"Did I hear you say you are going to the fire pit later?" she asks as she looks behind me. I frown as I follow her line of sight and can't see anything.

"Yeah, why?" I ask, wondering if there's a problem.

"Because I have a little idea that may make it even more special for Elli," she says with a wink. She quickly fills me in on a conversation she had with Elli whilst I was out. I smile down at her before planting a kiss on her cheek.

"You are a genius, Mom," I whisper as I walk away from her, looking forward to spending the evening just Elli, me and a little surprise.

Elli

I have had such a lovely day with Luke's mum and sisters. I had been so worried that they wouldn't like me, but they've been so welcoming. Luke's mum has let me help her with the food and preparing everything for the evening meal. She taught me how to make dinner rolls, and I promised to teach her how to make mincemeat which will go into the mince pies I make in a couple of days.

Rachel took me to the house Billy, Luke and their dad had built for them. It's beautiful, a little smaller than what they call the main house where the family live. Billy and Rachel always knew they wanted to bring up any kids they may have on the ranch. Who can blame them? This is the perfect place for kids to grow up. Skyla is so adventurous and outgoing; I know they'll have their hands full as she gets older.

Everything about today has been perfect. As soon as we finished eating dinner, Annie declared that Luke and I were to go on ahead and leave as Luke wanted to take me somewhere and that Lily and Billy would help with the dishes. Luke grabbed my hand and pulled me out of there as quickly as possible, saying he knows I'll refuse to leave without helping somehow; I guess he knows me better than I thought!

We're now walking through the woods not far from the house. Luke leads the way with a bright torch in one hand, the other gripped tightly to mine.

"Are you sure it's safe to be out here? Don't you have bears and stuff in Alabama?" I ask nervously as Luke laughs next to me.

"I promise you're safer here than you are in Chicago on a night out," he states as he gives my hand a quick squeeze. "We have black bears in Alabama, and they are more scared of you than you are of them," he adds calmly. I look at him with raised brows.

"I beg to differ. They terrify the shit out of me."

Luke laughs and lets go of my hand so he can put an arm around my shoulders.

"I promise if we encounter any bears or coyotes, I will protect you," he chuckles as he pulls me closer.

"My hero!" I sigh, sarcastically rolling my eyes. Luke chuckles again, shaking his head.

"I think you will forget all about them in a minute

anyway," Luke says as he guides me through some trees into a clearing, and I feel his arm slip from around my shoulders.

I stop in my tracks as there, in the middle of the clearing, is a circle of rocks; a fire ring already stocked with fresh wood. Around the ring are cut-down tree trunks. But what stops me is the view above us. When I look up, I can see more stars than I have ever seen in my life.

"It's beautiful," I whisper as I slowly turn a complete 360, trying to see as much as possible. I look towards the fire pit, where I find Luke lighting the fire. I walk over to him and sit down on one of the logs and watch as he has the fire going in no time.

"You planned this little trip earlier, didn't you?" I ask as I notice the wood still looks new and dry. Luke turns around and smiles at me with that cheeky grin.

"I may have thought ahead a little," he replies with a wink before sitting next to me. He places the bag he's been carrying in front of him and opens it carefully. He reaches inside and pulls out two beer bottles before producing a Swiss army knife from his pocket. He finds the bottle opener and pops off the caps and puts them in the front pocket of his bag. I take the bottle he hands me and hold it out to him.

"Cheers, cowboy," I say happily as he taps his against mine.

"Cheers, legs," he replies, looking just as happy as I feel.

We sit in silence for a moment watching the fire roar and drinking our drinks. I look up occasionally and watch the stars. A few times, I close my eyes and take deep breaths, smelling all the scents around me. I can smell the wood burning and the trees around us all mixed with Luke's intoxicating scent of sawdust and aftershave. The air is so much fresher here than in the city. There is minimal sound, which makes it even more relaxing. Besides the crackling of the wood burning and the crickets chirping, there's the occasional howling sound, which Luke informs me are coyotes. He promises that they are pretty far away and no threat to us. I believe him, but that doesn't mean I don't jump the first few times I hear them.

After enjoying the peace and silence, I hear Luke rummaging around in his bag. I look at him as he drops something on my knee.

"Open them up for us, legs."

I frown as I look down and see a packet of marshmallows. I turn to Luke as I feel the biggest smile spread on my face as he holds up a chocolate bar and some graham crackers. "I hear you've never made s'mores," Luke says with a massive grin. I squeal excitedly, bouncing where I sit like an eager puppy.

"Okay, you have to show me how to do this!" I beg as I open the bag, quickly grab a marshmallow, and shove it in my mouth.

"You know you are meant to roast them first, right?" Luke asks with arched brows.

"I'm just checking they're okay," I mumble with a mouth full of marshmallows as I shrug.

"And are they?" he asks. I can see he's trying to keep a straight face, but it isn't working.

"I don't know. I need to check once more," I answer as I grab one out of the bag at the same time as Luke pulls the bag out of my reach. "Hey, no fair!" I protest. But Luke stares at me with that lopsided smile he gets.

"Do you want to try s'mores or not?" he asks; I nod eagerly. "Then stop eating all the marshmallows, legs," he says as he shakes his head, and he pushes a marshmallow onto a stick.

"Have you at least roasted marshmallows?" Luke asks; I shake my head.

"Damn, legs, I'm gonna have to teach you everything. Now hold this over the fire, and slowly rotate it like this," he puts the stick into my hand and then guides me through what to do.

"Now, slowly pull the stick out. I will hold the crackers, so the marshmallow stays in them." I do as he tells me to. "There you go, you just made your first s'more. Now give it a try," Luke says as he hands it to me. I look at the side of it and see the chocolate has melted and mixed with the marshmallow. I look at Luke, who is watching me with a grin on his face. I take a deep breath and bite into the s'more. As the flavours hit my mouth, I look back at Luke with wide eyes.

"This is amazing!" I exclaim with my hand over my mouth, Luke chuckles at me, spearing another marshmallow with the stick.

"I'm glad you like it, want another one?" he asks. I nod eagerly as I finish the one in my hand and watch him make more.

Chapter Ten

LUKE

Elli and I stay by the fire until the embers are almost out; I pour some water on it and make sure it is safe to leave before packing up and heading back home. It's nearly ten by the time we get back, and the house is in darkness. We sneak up the stairs as quietly as possible, and make our way to my room. Both giggling as soon as we're inside, like a couple of teenagers sneaking in after a late-night party.

I walk out of the en-suite a few minutes later as Elli grabs her pyjamas and goes in. As I reflect on the evening, I change out of my jeans and into some sweatpants in the bedroom.

I had the most fantastic time with Elli tonight. Within moments of reaching the fire pit, Elli relaxed, and for a while, I witnessed the stress from the last few months melt away. There were moments she would sit there with her eyes closed, listening and breathing deeply, and I couldn't tear my eyes away from her. Elli is always gorgeous but seeing her in the light from the fire and with the stars twinkling in her eyes tonight was genuinely breath-taking. I don't think I have ever seen anything as beautiful as she looked this evening.

I'm chucking a pillow onto the couch when I hear the en-suite door opening. I turn to see Elli walking into the room, brushing her hair. She looks at me, setting up the couch and frowns.

"I meant to ask, where did you sleep last night?"

I smile sheepishly at her as I answer, "I fell asleep whilst we were talking, so on the bed with you, sorry," I wait for her to get annoyed, but instead, she shrugs.

"You might as well sleep on the bed tonight then. Seems pointless you sleeping on the couch now," she says as she climbs into bed. I look at her for a moment.

"Don't worry, cowboy. I'm not going to jump you," she adds with an eye roll. I can't help laughing as I climb onto the bed next to her, being sure to leave a gap between us.

Elli rolls on her side like last night and places her hands under her head.

"Thank you for tonight. I had a great time," she whispers, looking at me with the sweetest smile. I turn to face her.

"I had a great time too. Maybe we can do it again tomorrow?" I ask nervously. Elli's face lights up as she nods.

"I'd like that," she whispers as she yawns. "Night, cowboy," she mumbles as she closes her eyes and rolls onto her back, placing her left hand in the gap between us.

"Sweet dreams, legs," I whisper back as I roll over and switch the bedside lamp off. I settle onto my back, leaving one hand not far from hers, the other behind my head.

I lay in the dark, listening to Elli breathing lightly beside me. After spending time away from work and the city, I realise my feelings for Elli go deeper than I initially thought. This woman is amazing, and I look forward to every second

I get to spend with her. I know she must feel something too. The chemistry between us is like nothing I've ever felt before. But I don't know how to explain it to her. What if I'm looking into this more than I should? What if I say something and she doesn't feel the same? Would we continue this charade that we are a couple? Or would she pack up and head back to the city?

I'm not used to this feeling of uncertainty. I don't date because I have no idea when it comes to women, and to be honest, I've always been happy with my own company. That was until I met this amazing woman next to me, and somehow in the last six months, I started caring more about her than I have anyone outside of my family. But for the last two days, she has become part of that family, and I want to keep her there.

I hear Elli murmur something in her sleep as she rolls onto her side, facing me. But as she does, her hand falls on top of mine, and I feel her interlock our fingers, so she's holding my hand. I look down and see she's fast asleep, looking so peaceful. I roll onto my side, not letting go of her hand as I reach over with the other to brush some hair off her face gently.

"Go to sleep, cowboy. I can hear you thinking, and it's keeping me awake," She murmurs as I see the glimpse of a smile on her face, as her fingers tighten around mine. I smile as I lift her hand to my mouth and press a kiss to it.

"Sorry, legs. I'll sleep now," I whisper as I close my eyes, feeling like tomorrow could bring something good for the two of us.

Chapter Eleven

LUKE

I look up from the fence I'm fixing with Pops and watch Elli as she plays with Skyla. They've been running around, skipping and playing hopscotch all day. Elli has snuck them some cookies, and they are sitting under one of the big trees, eating them as they giggle together.

"She's a good'un son." I turn at my father's voice. He's leaning against the fence I'm fixing, watching his granddaughter with a smile on his face.

"That she is Pops," I reply before returning to the wooden plank I'm sawing.

"Why don't you go and spend more time with her rather than fixing this? We manage just fine when you aren't here. You don't have to come back and help out," he says as he holds the plank I've just cut against the post so I can nail it in to place.

"I know that, but I want to do all this stuff. I miss it," I admit, trying to avoid looking at my father as I know he'll be smirking. He always said I would miss ranch life, and I just proved him right.

"Then why stay in the city? Come home if you miss it. Or are you staying for a certain little lady?" I look over at Elli and smile as I catch her looking back at me.

"She might have something to do with it. I didn't realise it before," I answer honestly.

"I don't know the deal with you two, but whatever you have going on means a lot to you both. You can see it in the way you look at each other. Maybe you need to sit down and ask her what she wants," Pops suggests. He's always been able to read me better than anyone.

"Elli wants to be the best at what she does. She's competitive and driven to succeed. She deserves more than just a cowboy," I sigh.

"There's more to us than fixing fences and herding cattle; you know that. Since you were knee-high to a grasshopper, you've worried that you're not good enough, but I'm telling you this for nothing, to that young lady over there, you are *more* than enough. She's stealing as many glances at you as you are at her. She's been watching you work this whole time, and who can blame her? You're a good-looking lad," Pops chuckles. I look at him, smirking before shaking my head as I go back to nailing the plank.

"I know you think I'm as old as dirt and have no idea what I'm talking about, but I think you'll find Elli's seeing a different side to you here and likes it. You're seeing a different side to her too, and you both may need to consider that you could be happier here than in the city. Together, you could make anywhere home."

"You miss me being around to fix your fences and do all the woodwork. I've seen Billy's attempt to fix that shed over there. Skyla would have done a better job," I laugh. Pops chuckles as he looks at me.

"Yeah, you have a certain skill when it comes to

anything wooden. But that's not why I want you to consider coming home. You sound downright miserable when we speak. The only time your mood seems to pick up is when you mention Elli over there. That can't be a coincidence. Plus, your mom misses you. We all do."

I'm just about to reply when we both turn to the sound of a pickup coming down the road. I recognise it straight away and smile. I quickly hammer in the last nail and stand up. I'm wiping the dust off my jeans when the pickup stops in front of us, and a large blonde-haired man climbs out of the driver's side door.

"You've been home forty-eight hours and haven't even bothered to call! I'm hurt, brother," Mitch calls as he walks toward Pops and me. I laugh as I shake his hand and pull him in for a one-armed hug.

"What can I say? I've been busy," I reply, stepping back.

"From what I hear, you've been busy with your city girl. You hiding her from us, or what?" My other friend, Dan, calls as he walks over from the pick-up. I laugh before shaking his hand and hugging him too.

"Who told you about Elli?" I ask, grinning.

"Oh, that's her name? Brother, the whole town's talking about how you two were seen acting like a couple of lovesick teenagers yesterday. That her up yonder?" He asks as he nods towards the girls. I look over and see Elli drawing something with Skyla.

"Yeah, that's her," I reply quietly. "Hey legs, come here a minute," I yell. Elli looks up before getting to her feet and heading over to us. Pops leaves us to join Skyla. As soon as Elli's next to me, I place an arm around her shoulders and pull her close. She instantly leans into me and places a hand on my stomach.

"Elli, these two morons are my oldest friends; Mitch,

and Dan," I say as both take off their hats and take turns to shake her hand.

"Hi, it's nice to meet you," Elli says, smiling at them.

"The pleasure's all ours, ma'am. Are you British?" Mitch asks, his eyes bulging. Elli laughs, nodding.

"Sure am," she answers as both guys turn and look at me, smirking.

"Luke, you lucky son of a bitch," Dan curses before apologising to Elli.

"It's fine; I've heard and said worse," she giggles.

"Yeah, usually at me," I chuckle as I smile at her.

"And yet you still steal my coffee," she replies, shrugging, as I kiss the top of her head.

"Yep," I clap back as I look at my friends, who are both grinning.

"Well, we came to drag you out for a few drinks. We're not taking no for an answer," Mitch grins.

"Ah, man, I can't. We've got to sort out some stuff for work," I sigh. Elli and I decided this morning to do some work over a few beers tonight instead of going to the fire pit.

"We can leave it for one more night. Go and have a few drinks with your mates," Elli says as I frown at her.

"But we haven't done anything on it since we arrived," I point out, but Elli shrugs.

"So? We still have plenty of time, go and have fun," she replies with a smile.

"You make it sound like I would leave you here! If I'm going out, you're coming too," I answer with an arched brow.

"Damn straight, I bet you can be real fun after a few drinks," Dan says, grinning at her.

"You bet I can," Elli says excitedly. I chuckle as I tighten my arm around her shoulders and am surprised when she slips her hand into the back pocket of my jeans.

"That's sorted then. Grab your shit; we're heading off in five minutes," Mitch exclaims as he rubs his hands together. Elli and I both laugh and go to head into the house.

As soon as we are in the bedroom, I take Elli's hand and pull her back, so she's facing me.

"We don't have to go out with them if you don't want to. I can tell them no," I point out as I look into her hazel eyes. But Elli smiles up at me, her whole face brightening.

"Maybe I want to go out and have a few drinks with you and your mates. You told me you want to know all about me. Maybe I want to know all about you too, especially what you were like before moving to the city," Elli states before kissing me on the cheek. "Plus, I think drunk you could be fun," she adds with a wink before walking off towards the en-suite. My heart racing as I watch her. Fuck, I'm falling for this woman, and hard.

Chapter Twelve

ELLI

We've been in the bar for a few hours, and my face and stomach hurt from laughing. Mitch and Dan are a blast; I can see why the three guys have been friends for so long.

Over the last three days, I've seen a different side to Luke that takes my breath away. Watching him work on the ranch is an entirely different experience than watching him work from my desk on our company's floor. It's a real treat to the eye seeing him in a shirt and trousers but watching him in those jeans and fitted t-shirts are just something else. I could watch him all day, to see those muscles flex and roll across his broad shoulders and down his arms, and don't get me started on his back and abs. Damn, that man puts every guy I have ever met to shame.

The four of us are sitting in a booth. I'm next to Luke, who has his arm around the back behind me. Now and again, I feel him play with my hair or run his fingers across my shoulder, and it sends shock waves to my core every time. I swear he knows what he's doing as he keeps smirking at me as his eyes darken.

As Dan and Mitch get up and leave us for a moment, Luke turns in his seat to face me and smiles.

"What you smiling at, cowboy?" I ask, grinning, feeling a little tipsy and very brave.

"You. I don't think I've ever seen you laugh and smile as much as you have the last few days," he replies. I shrug as I take a sip of my beer.

"Maybe I'm happier than usual," I tease as I look up at him through my lashes. Luke stares at me, and his smile widens further as he leans in to whisper in my ear.

"And why are you so happy?" he asks, his warm breath tickling against my skin. God, I'm so horny right now. I lean back a little so that I can look into his eyes.

"Maybe I'm enjoying a certain cowboy's company," I reply bravely. Luke leans in a little closer, and I can see him looking at my mouth, I slowly bite my bottom lip, and I swear he takes a sharp intake of breath.

"I think I'm seeing a new side to you this week, legs. One I like a lot," he whispers into my ear as I feel his lips lightly brush against my neck. I turn my head to the side, and our eyes lock. I stare into them for a moment and feel the urge to lean forward to kiss him. But would he kiss me back? His body language is screaming yes, but I'm tipsy and could be seeing what's not there.

"You two need to get a room because the whole place is watching you."

I quickly turn my head and see Mitch grinning at us as he puts a tray of drinks on the table, killing the moment. I look around and see he isn't lying. Everyone's watching us, and I feel my cheeks burning with embarrassment. Luke chuckles next to me and turns back to face the table as he again puts his arm on the back of the booth. We are sitting hip to hip, and neither of us makes any move to put any distance between us.

I look down at Mitch's tray on the table and see four beers plus four shot glasses.

"Do I even want to ask what they are?" I say, pointing to the tray. The guys all chuckle around me.

"It's a tradition that we have a shot of tequila before our last beer of the night," Dan says as he returns from the bar.

"So what are those for?" Luke asks, pointing to the shot glasses in Dan's hands. Mitch and Dan both smile at each other before looking back at us.

"These are to celebrate you finally finding a woman as beautiful and funny as El," Mitch adds with a wink.

"What if Elli doesn't drink tequila?" Luke asks. I turn in my seat frowning.

"Are you trying to steal my drink?" I ask. Luke looks at me, still grinning.

"I risk my life enough every day by stealing your coffee. I ain't brave enough to steal your drink, too," he chuckles before looking deep into my eyes. "I'm just wondering if you can handle any more," he adds.

I reach out until I feel a shot glass in my hand, refusing to look away from the challenge in Luke's eyes. I bring the glass to my lips and tip my head back, allowing the liquid to slide across my tongue and down my throat, making a point of him seeing me swallow. I take the cowboy hat off his head that he's been wearing all day and place it on my own.

"You'd be surprised how much I can handle, cowboy," I say with a wink before turning back to the table and picking up my beer bottle and taking a deep drink. Mitch and Dan are staring at me with huge grins on their faces.

"Luke, I've said it once, and I will say it a thousand times, you lucky son of a bitch," Dan laughs as he holds his bottle out for me, and I clink mine against it. This time, when Luke puts his arm around the back of our seat, he lets it fall, so his arm is around the bottom of my back, and his hand is resting on my hip.

"If you ever get bored of him, you come and find me, Elli, and I'll show you a good time," Dan says with a wink. I feel Luke's hand tighten possessively on my hip to the point that I'm sure it will leave a bruise. I lean in against him and smile at his friend.

"I'm fine, but thanks for the offer," I say as I feel Luke's grip loosen and his hand slides up to my waist. As Luke chuckles, I feel his thumb rubbing lightly against my side. I place my hand on his knee and grin as I feel his thumb falter for a moment. Fuck, I want this man. I need him so bad.

"I don't think Luke will be letting Elli go any time soon, Dan," Mitch chuckles as he holds his shot out to Luke, who clinks his own against it before necking it. Luke looks down at me and smiles before turning back to Dan.

"Nope, now I've got her. I don't think I'll ever let her go."

Chapter Thirteen

LUKE

I catch Elli as she falls out of my brother's truck, giggling.

"How much did you guys drink?" Billy sighs as he climbs out of the driver's side, staring at Elli and me as we chuckle together.

"I think the third shot may have been a bad idea," I laugh as Elli stands up and looks at me with her hands on her hips, my hat still on her head.

"Speak for yourself, cowboy; I'm fine," she states with the slightest slur to her voice before turning to Billy.

"Thanks for picking us up. Sorry if we woke you," she says, smiling at him as she leans against his truck. He shakes his head, letting out a deep laugh.

"Elli, you are more than welcome, but this is as far as I'm taking you. You need to get yourself up to his room."

I look at Elli and realise she's leaning on the truck for a little more support than I initially thought. She turns to face the house and I can see she's wondering if she can make it. I look at Billy, who's grinning at her. He glances at me, and I roll my eyes whilst shaking my head.

"Okay, legs. Up you go," I sigh as I spin Elli around, pick her up, and throw her over my shoulder.

"What the hell?" Elli screeches as she throws her hand up to stop my hat from falling off her head. Billy roars laughing as I turn to face him, grinning.

"See you in the morning, Billy," I call as I salute and turn back towards the main house.

"Luke, you better put me down," Elli hisses through her teeth. I don't slow my pace as I reach the porch.

"I will when I get you to the room. Unless you think you can walk there on your own without falling over or waking anyone up?" I chuckle. Elli goes still on my shoulder, and I feel my hat returning to my head.

"Point made, cowboy," she whispers, quickly followed by a hiccup that makes me chuckle harder.

I walk into the house and quickly head to the bedroom, hoping we haven't already woken Pops up. As we get to the top of the stairs, the bathroom door opens, and Grams walks out. I freeze where I'm standing, with Elli still over my shoulder and look at my ninety-year-old Grandmother, staring at us with the biggest eyes before a huge smile spreads across her face.

I lower Elli down slowly and turn her so she faces Grams. I wrap an arm around her waist and pull her against me, so her back is pressed to my front.

"It's not what it looks like," Elli says quickly as she leans back into me further, and I have to stop us from toppling down the stairs.

"It looks like you had a good time. See you both in the morning," Grams replies with a smile as she walks into her room, chuckling to herself.

"Night, Grams," I whisper as Elli spins around and hides her face in my chest, obviously embarrassed. I chuckle as I nudge her towards the back of the house where our room is.

As soon as we're inside, Elli removes her hands from her face and looks at me, her cheeks rosy from a combination of the alcohol and embarrassment. She looks so cute that I can't stop myself from placing a hand against her cheek and running a thumb over it. I watch as her eyes close, and she leans into my touch.

"God, I want to kiss you," I whisper as I step closer to her. Elli doesn't open her eyes, but I can't miss the deep breath she takes. "There are so many things I want to do to you. I want to see you under, on top, and in front of me on your hands and knees. I want to hear you scream my name as you climax over and over again," I whisper as Elli opens her eyes and looks at me.

"Luke," Elli gasps as she steps forward, closing the gap between us and threading her arms around my neck; I lean down and stop as my lips brush against hers slightly.

"But I won't, not tonight," I whisper.

"Why?" Elli asks just as quietly.

"Because I don't want there to be any doubts between us. I want you to be sure this is what you want when I take you, baby," I whisper as I lean my head to the side and let my lips brush against her neck.

"Did you just call me, baby?" she gasps.

"Do you like it?" I whisper against her skin as she groans, leaning into me further. With every moan that escapes her, I feel myself getting harder.

"Yes," Elli gasps as I let my lips softly slide up her neck and come to a stop by her ear. I thread my fingers into her hair and the top of her neck and pull her head back, exposing her neck further.

"Baby, you have no idea what you do to me. I need you

so bad, but I won't ruin this before we can see where it could go," I whisper as I kiss her neck and hear her groan again. "I don't want to wake up in the morning and you to look at me with regret in your eyes. I won't lose you. You're too important and precious to me," I explain as I kiss her jawline.

"I won't regret it," she gasps as I kiss the side of her lips. I look deep into her eyes and feel myself harden to the point that it's painful.

"Then you can wait until tomorrow night when I promise if you still want me, I will take you to highs you have only ever dreamt of. I will fuck you until you beg me to stop, and then I will make love to you until we are both spent and can't do anything but sleep in each other's arms," I whisper as I stand tall and look into her eyes. "Go to sleep, legs; we will revisit this conversation tomorrow, sober," I lean down and kiss her on the cheek before walking towards the en-suite to give us a little space and to have an icy shower.

"Just so you know, cowboy, it will be worth the wait," I hear Elli chuckle as she walks over to the bed and pulls off her top. I have to force myself to keep walking away from her and close the bathroom door between us.

As soon as I'm inside, I lean against the door and take a deep breath. Fuck, the things that woman does to me are like nothing I've ever felt before. I knew I had feelings for her from the day we met but being here with her makes me realise I'm in deep shit because the longer we are here, the less likely it is that we can ever go back to the way things were for us before.

I walk to the shower and turn it on, quickly setting the water to cold. I release my dick from the restraint of my jeans and look down at myself. I swear I've never been as hard as I am right now. I quickly take off the rest of my clothes and step under the water. The cold spray hits me but does nothing to soften my rock-hard cock. I take it in my hand and stroke it once, twice, and I swear I'm already close to falling apart; I hear the softest moan come from the bedroom and imagine Elli lying on my bed, feeling herself, hoping to find her own release as I stand under this water trying to do the same.

The image of her lying there, legs spread, finger fucking herself, the other hand squeezing her nipple, as she thinks of me, has me stroking myself harder and faster. I picture it all in my mind as she releases her nipple and starts flicking her clit as she continues to finger herself, getting harder and faster as she bites on her bottom lip to stop herself from moaning, hoping I won't know what she's doing to release the built-up sexual frustration that's been growing between us all night.

I place a hand against the cold, wet tiles as I look down, the water spraying onto my head and running over my back and shoulders as I continue to stroke myself. I hear another moan from the bedroom and feel a groan escape my lips in response. I'm so close now, and I feel my cock harden to the point I gasp in pain. For the first time, I truly understand the term blue balls. Because I swear that if I don't find my release soon, I will scream in pain and frustration.

I'm so close to climaxing; the image of Elli pushes me closer and closer to the edge. I'm right there when I hear my name from the bedroom in a tone that only confirms Elli is masturbating on my bed.

"Fuck, Luke," I hear her gasp as she pushes herself over the edge. It's my undoing, and I fall apart as I growl her name and release the biggest load I've ever seen. I swear I cum so hard I see stars. I continue to hold myself up by leaning against the tiles, gasping for breath and unable to concentrate on anything other than keeping myself upright on my shaky legs.

A few minutes later, I switch off the shower and step out before wrapping a towel around my waist. I quickly dry myself off and pull on the sweatpants I left in here this morning.

I walk into the bedroom to find Elli asleep on the bed. Her amber hair is sprayed across the pillow, and she looks peaceful. I lean down and gently kiss the top of her head, making her moan slightly in her sleep. I can't help myself; I kiss her again and whisper in her ear.

"Sweet dreams, baby," before standing up and walking over to the other side. I slide under the covers and curl up on my side facing her as I fall into a deep, peaceful sleep.

Chapter Fourteen

ELLI

I turn over in bed to find Luke has already gone again. I roll onto my back and moan as I remember last night. Why do I always think tequila is a good idea? I never learn it makes me horny and gives me a killer headache the following day? I turn to face the bathroom door and flashback to last night after we returned.

Even over the shower, I could hear Luke as he moaned with pleasure, and I couldn't stop myself from joining in. He had left me so sexually frustrated that there was no way I could've gone to sleep. Knowing how thin the wall between the en-suite and the bedroom is, I knew he would hear everything. I'd made sure of it. I heard him growl my name as he came. That growl had nearly pushed me over the edge a second time. There was something so masculine and dominating about it. But was it all just the drink talking? Last night when he spoke of not wanting any regret between us, I thought he was talking about me, but what if he meant himself?

I sit on the edge of the bed and hold my head in my

hands. Damn Tequila! I look to the side for my phone and find a piece of paper, a glass of water and two tablets on the bedside cabinet. I smile as I pick up the note and instantly recognise Luke's handwriting.

Morning legs,
I hope you don't feel too rough. I've left some water and aspirin for you in case you need them.
Everyone is out running errands. I'll be out seeing to a few jobs that need doing. Text me when you're up, and I'll come back.
I'll make sure there is coffee in the pot for you.
Yours
Luke xx

I smile as I reread the note before putting it down to take the tablets. I look towards the bathroom and jump up, eager to get washed, dressed and out there to find out what Luke's up to.

Twenty minutes later, I'm walking out of the house with a mug of coffee in one hand and my phone in the other as I quickly text him.

Elli: Morning, cowboy. I'm up, showered, dressed, and drinking coffee. How long do you think you will be? Xx

I don't have to wait long for a reply.

Luke: Won't be long. Are you missing me, legs? Xx

Elli: That would be telling. Xx

Luke: I'll take that as a Yes. I'll be back in five. Xx

I look up and wonder what to do with myself until he returns. I walk around the side of the house, where I haven't been before, thinking it would be the back garden. But instead, I find three of the most beautiful horses I've ever seen.

I slowly walk up to the paddock, and they move away from me; all bar one. A light brown horse with the silkiest white hair approaches me. It's tan all over except for its two front feet and what looks like a white splat mark on its back. It's so adorable.

"Well, hey there, handsome," I say softly as I hold out my hand and wait to see if it will let me stroke it. Almost instantly, it sniffs my hand and rubs against it. "Well, aren't you just the most beautiful horse I've ever seen?" I gush over it as I continue to stroke its head.

"I see you found Mitzy," I turn to find Luke walking towards me in his wool-lined denim jacket, jeans, and boots.

"She's beautiful," I reply with a smile as I turn back to the horse, nudging me for attention.

"She's not the only one," Luke whispers as he places a kiss on my cheek before leaning against the fence next to me. I can feel my cheeks blushing with embarrassment. As the other horses notice him, they rush up, nudging him for attention.

"Never put you down as a horse lover," he chuckles as a black and white horse tries to get at his hat.

"Never been this close to one before," I admit, still stroking Mitzy.

"Never?" Luke asks, sounding amazed. I shake my head as I answer.

"Nope, never. I always wanted to go horse riding but

never got the chance," I answer as I giggle at Luke, fighting to keep his hat on his head and out of the other horse's mouth.

"Seriously? Well, now I know what we're doing today," he replies as he walks up to me and takes my hand before he pulls me towards the large barn.

"Where are we going?" I ask as I hurry to keep up with him. Luke pulls me into the stables, where he lets go of my hand and picks up a saddle.

"You're going to ride a horse," he announces, grinning at me. I freeze and stare back at the horses.

"What? Now?" I ask as I become stuck to the spot with nerves. Luke steps towards me, places a finger under my chin and tilts my head back so I'm looking into his eyes.

"Do you trust me?" he asks. I don't hesitate and nod instantly. Luke looks down at me and smiles before kissing me on the cheek again. "Then let's teach you to ride so I can show you our lands," he says as he takes the saddle, and we walk out to the back of the stables and into the paddock where the three horses are. Luke whistles, and all three rush over. He lets go of my hand and starts petting Mitzy.

"Mitzy is the perfect horse for your first ride. She's soft-tempered and doesn't like to go fast," he explains as I see him throw a blanket over her back and then place the saddle on top. I watch as he expertly gets the horse ready. He turns to see me watching and smiles.

"Next time, I'll get you to saddle up yourself. I'll turn you into a pro in no time," he says, grinning. He looks so happy. I can't help feeling excited myself.

Luke

I take Elli's hand and Mitzy's reins and walk them to the paddock's edge. I can tell Elli's nervous as well as excited. I tie Mitzy to the fence before turning to Elli and placing a hand on her hip, pulling her closer to me.

"Remember everything I told you?" I ask. Elli nods and bites her bottom lip nervously. I use my thumb to prise the lip from between her teeth before cupping her cheek in my hand.

"I'll be right here next to you the whole time. Nothing will ever harm you when you're with me, that I can promise you," I say as I look into her hazel eyes, which seem to sparkle a little more each day we are here.

"I know," Elli whispers. I can't stop myself from leaning in and placing a soft kiss on her lips. That this fantastic woman trusts me implicitly means more than I could ever put into words.

"Come on, then. Let's get you up on this horse," I say with a smile as I turn her around to face Mitzy. Surprisingly Elli gets up onto the saddle quickly the first time. I stand beside her with a hand on her leg while she gets herself comfortable and her feet into the stirrups.

"How do you feel?" I ask as I look up at her excited smile.

"Good," she answers as she leans forward and runs a hand down the back of Mitzy's head. "You won't throw me off, will ya girl?" she asks the horse, chuckling. I walk in front of Mitzy and run a hand down her nose.

"She won't if she knows what's good for her," I say as I look up at Elli. She looks so beautiful up on the back of my favourite horse; it was like she was meant to be there. "Ready?" I ask. Elli nods and takes a deep breath as she takes the reins I hand her, and nods again. "Come on then," I call, grinning as I lead them into the centre of the paddock.

An hour later, I'm leaning against the fence, smiling as I watch Mitzy and Elli trot around the paddock on their own. As I thought, Elli's a natural on a horse. You'd think she'd been riding her whole life. Maybe Pops was right; maybe we could have a life here together. I can see Elli fitting in perfectly with ranch life; she's already fitted into our family. Everyone has told me how much they love her and all nervousness she displayed when we arrived seems to have disappeared.

"Oi, cowboy!"

I smile as Elli trots up to me. I step in front of Mitzy and take the reins, getting her to stop.

"Had enough, legs?" I ask as I look up. Her hair's a little windswept, and her cheeks have that rosy, red look about them again.

"Yeah, I need a coffee. How do I get down?" she asks, looking at the ground. I laugh as I walk to the horse's side and stand facing her.

"Put both your legs this side, and I'll help you," I instruct.

Elli carefully lifts her right leg and swings it over Mitzy's back, so she's sitting facing me. I stand directly in front of her and place my hands on her thighs. "Now, slowly lower yourself, and I'll catch you." Elli looks down nervously, and I squeeze her thighs slightly. "Look at me," I say softly. She does, and I smile at her, "I won't let you fall." Elli nods and starts to lower herself from the saddle. I let my hands slide up her thighs, over her hips and to her waist, where I tighten my hold, taking her weight before lowering her down to her feet.

As soon as her feet touch the floor, I feel her legs wobble underneath her, and I press her against me to hold her up.

"Jelly legs?" I ask, grinning.

"Just a bit," she replies, giggling as she puts her arms around my neck like last night. I look into her eyes and grin. She looks so happy and carefree; it's a look that suits her. I look deep into her eyes and lower my head until I feel her lips against mine, she doesn't pull back, so I tighten my hold on her back and press her closer to me. Elli's fingers thread into the hair at the base of my head as I run my tongue over her lips which part willingly, the kiss deepens, and we quickly lose ourselves in each other's touch.

"I hope you're not making out against my prize mare!"

We both jump apart and look to where Pops is walking towards us, Billy beside him, grinning like a fool.

"Well, we're not now," I call back as Elli buries her face with her hands into my chest, hiding with embarrassment. I laugh as I tighten my arms around her shoulder and kiss the top of her head. "We're taking Mitzy and Reggie out for the day," I call back as they come closer to us. Elli looks at me, frowning.

"No problem, we don't need them. Where are you going?" Pops asks as he leans against the fence with Billy next to him. Elli turns in my arms to face them, and I wrap my arms around her, keeping her close to me.

"I'm going to show Elli the lands and then take her to the lake," I answer, looking at Pops, who smiles knowingly.

"Sounds like a great plan. Have you ever ridden a horse before, Elli?" Pop asks. Elli nods in my arms.

"I have now. Luke's spent the morning teaching me on Mitzy," she replies.

"Elli's a natural," I add as she looks up over her shoulder at me, smiling.

My dad and Billy say a quick goodbye, and both head off towards the goats whilst I pull Elli into the house.

"Go get a warmer jacket, and I'll fill the flask and chuck some food in a bag. I'll meet you back by the horses," I say as I push her towards the stairs. Elli looks at me excitedly before rushing off, taking the stairs two at a time. I watch her go with a massive grin on my face looking forward to showing her my favourite spot on our lands.

Chapter Fifteen

ELLI

We've been riding for hours. The land owned by Luke's family is enormous. They have goats, cattle, and more horses than the three in the paddock. They also have chickens and pigs, as well as wheat and grass fields they turn into hay for the livestock. Luke gets so animated when he talks about the ranch and what they do from one season to the next; I honestly don't understand why he left this life to move to the city.

Finally, we stop, and I look out over a vast lake; the water is clear and calm. Even in the chilly weather, it looks appealing, and I want to jump in and go for a swim.

"It's beautiful, is this yours as well?" I ask as Luke helps me down from Mitzy. He nods and looks down at me as he gives me time to find my legs again. After a moment, he takes my hand and gently pulls me away from the horses and towards the water's edge.

"This whole area used to belong to my Gramps. When he passed away, he left it to Pops, who has never found a use for it other than for fishing. I'm glad, as I think it's perfect the way it is," Luke says as he looks out at the clear blue water.

"I wouldn't change anything about it," I sigh as I look around. Luke moves to stand behind me and wraps his arms around my waist. I place my hands on his, resting on my stomach and lean back into him, feeling more content each time he holds me.

"I would change a couple of things," Luke whispers as he rests his chin on my right shoulder.

"Like what?" I ask, leaning my cheek against his. He turns us slightly and points to a clear piece of land directly in front of the lake.

"I'd build a house over there and a fire pit where we're standing so I could sit out here in the evening and eat s'mores and listen to the wildlife," he says softly. I look around and can picture the type of house I would have, one just like Rachel and Billy's.

"That sounds amazing," I sigh as I lean into him. I have to stop myself from asking if I could visit. I don't know what this is between us yet. But I know that if I were lucky enough to be the girl Luke wanted to spend the rest of his life with, I certainly wouldn't turn down living in a place like this.

Luke

Elli and I stayed down by the lake until around three. I loved showing her this area, and I could picture us sitting together in the evenings as we got older. Would Elli leave the city for me? I don't know, but I like to think that what we've started here in Alabama will grow into something magical and meaningful when we return to the city. Who knows what the future could hold for us?

Since the heated kiss in the paddock earlier, we've only shared short kisses or pecks on the cheek or head. But all I can think about is getting her back to our room and making love to her. By the time we get back to the house, it's almost four. We find Mom in the kitchen. She asked Elli where I had taken her and what she thought of horse riding. They were so deep in conversation that I took the chance to jump into the shower quickly.

I'm walking out of the en-suite into the bedroom with nothing but a towel around my waist when Elli walks through the door. She stops in her tracks and stares at me for a moment; the door still ajar behind her. I love how she looks at me at times like this when the passion is so visible in her eyes. She takes her bottom lip between her teeth and bites on it.

Slowly, I walk up, reach out over her head, and close the door. Leaving my hand against the door, I take a step forward and place a hand on her hip as I lean down, look her in the eye, and let my lips brush against hers slightly.

"If I remember rightly, we have a conversation from last night we need to finish," I whisper as I lean over, so my lips bush against her neck, which she exposes to me further as she moans. I tighten my grip on her hip and kiss her neck again.

"Tell me to stop, baby, and I will," I whisper.

"Don't stop," Elli gasps. I lift my head so I'm facing her.

"I want you so bad, Elli; I have since the first day I met you," I admit.

"Finally," she gasps as she thrusts her fingers into my hair and kisses me on the lips. Within seconds I have her back pressed against the door and my front against hers. I reach down, cup her ass, and lift her so she can wrap her legs around my waist. I turn around and start walking toward the bed. I break the kiss and grin at her.

"Told you I'd get your legs around me one day," I gloat. Elli grins at me with a naughty glint in her eye.

"Play your cards right, and it will happen again and again,"

I look at her with a raised brow. "Baby, I'm going to make you cum harder than you did last night, and more than once," I reply, grinning as I drop us both onto the bed, so I'm between her legs. I grind into her once, knowing she will feel how hard she has me.

"Fuck Luke, I need you," she gasps as she tips her head back, and I go back to kissing her neck. Suddenly there is a loud knocking at the door.

"Go away, Lily!" I shout, knowing full well who it'll be. I return to kissing Elli, who's grinning when the door flies open. Elli screams as I curse and spin around to stare at my sister, Elli's legs still wrapped around my waist.

"Get out!" I yell, pointing at the door, but Lily can't see me as she has her hands over her eyes.

"Guys, it's the middle of the day!" Lily groans.

"Lily, I swear I will throw your ass out!" I shout as I move off Elli, who's trying very hard not to laugh as I stare at my sister as I sit on the edge of the bed.

"Whatever," Lily sighs before turning around to face us. "Elli, get dressed. You're coming out with Rachel and me. We're going for food and drinks and leave in twenty minutes," Lily removes her hands from her face and looks at the pair of us.

"No men allowed. You can carry this on after we get back. If she can after how drunk we're going to be," she adds before spinning around and leaving the room. "Just so you know, it wasn't up for discussion, so hurry up," she adds as she closes the door, and I hear her walking away.

"Why the hell does my family keep interrupting us?" I ask, rubbing my face with my hand. Elli bursts out laughing as she sits up and kisses me on the shoulder before climbing off the bed. "Where the hell are you going?" I ask as I pull her onto my lap. "I haven't finished with you yet," I declare as I thread my fingers into her hair and press my lips to hers.

Elli moves so she's straddling my lap before breaking the kiss.

"You have two choices. Our first time can be rushed with the chance of your sister barging back in. *Or*, you can wait until tonight when I get back, and I promise I won't be too drunk and won't regret anything, and you can have my legs wrapped around any part of you, you want."

"Well, how can I refuse an offer like that?" I reply before kissing her until my sister comes banging on the door, giving Elli a ten-minute warning.

Chapter Sixteen

ELLI

The girls and I have been out for a couple of hours and are having the best time. Luke's also out with Billy, Dan and Mitch in another bar. He's messaged a few times to check on me, but Rachel's now confiscated my phone and won't let me have it until we meet with them to head back to the ranch. She doesn't get out much and doesn't plan on rushing back 'so that I can get my leg over.' I may have called her a spoilsport, which just earned me her best 'mum' look. I'm not going to lie; that was a scary look, and I haven't dared complain since.

The whole evening has been filled with laughter, dancing and karaoke. I honestly can't remember the last time I'd had so much fun when out. As much as I enjoy my nights out in Chicago, I never relax around Grace like I do Rachel and Lily. I don't have to pretend to be someone I'm not. The only thing that has put any dampener on our night has been the unwanted attention I've received from a local.

Lily and Rachel have both informed me that his name is

Robert. Apparently, Luke and he have a long history of not getting along.

"He's probably realised that if you are out with us, you must be with Luke, and now he will want to try and prise you away from him," Lily says as she sips her drink. Rachel looks at me and shakes her head.

"Or he just thinks you're pretty, and because every woman in this bar knows to keep away from him, he might stand a chance with you," Rachel sighs; as I scrunch my nose.

"I have no plans of going anywhere near him. He looks like a bloody dickhead."

Both women burst out laughing, as I frown at them.

"Sorry, it's your accent, honey; it sounds funny as hell when you insult somebody," Rachel says as she tries to keep a straight face. I roll my eyes and sip my beer.

We continue drinking for a bit and chatting. When it's my turn to buy the round, I head to the busy bar and wait to get the server's attention. I feel someone tap me on the shoulder; I turn to see the big lad with a skinhead who's been staring at me all night.

"Howdy, I thought I would introduce myself. I'm Robert."

"Hey," I reply before turning away.

"Well, you're not from around here; where you from, sweetheart?" he asks, not taking the hint.

"Chicago," I reply, not bothering to turn back around.

"No, you're not. You're British."

"No shit, Sherlock," I mutter before stepping away from him and moving closer to the bar.

"Hey, I was talking to you," I hear him call as he gets closer.

"That's why I moved," I reply, trying to get the barman's attention.

"So, why you here?" he asks. I sigh and turn around to face him. He's a little taller than me, but more Billy's build than Luke's. I honestly consider pushing him away from me, but Rachel has already warned me that he can get violent.

"Look, I'm sure you are a nice guy, but I'm here with my man's sisters for a few pre-Christmas drinks. I'm not interested in whatever you're offering. Have a good night," I say as nicely as I can before turning around and looking at the barman, whom I realise is watching us.

"Is he bothering you, ma'am?" he asks, nodding to Robert behind me.

"Not anymore," I reply as I sense Robert storm off.

"Well, watch your back with him. He doesn't like being told no. Especially as he's probably guessed you're Luke's girl," he warns as he takes the caps off the three bottles I've ordered.

"Thanks, I'll bare that in mind," I reply as I pass him the right cash and fight my way away from the bar to where the others are sitting. I pass them their bottles and slide back into the booth.

"Well, that Robert's a pleasure!" I moan, rolling my eyes.

"What? Did he speak to you?" Lily asks, her eyes bulging as she looks around. I nod and take a sip of my drink.

"It's fine. I told him to back off," I reply. Rachel laughs as she holds out her bottle, and I clink mine against it.

"Honey, people don't usually have the guts to stand up to him; they usually run and hide out of his line of sight. You're meant to be Luke's girl," she laughs, grinning at me. I shrug and lean back into my seat.

"I don't like people getting in my face and assuming I want to talk to them. Hopefully, he'll stop staring at me from across the room now and move on to another victim," I say, as the hairs stand up on the back of my neck. "Or not," I mutter as I look behind me. In the corner of the bar is Robert staring at me; I roll my eyes and look back to Rachel and Lily, whom both realise he's watching.

"Want to drink up and go find the guys? We can have a few drinks with them before we finish for the night," Rachel asks. I nod and take another sip of my drink.

"Sounds like a great idea. That guy is pissing me off," I sigh.

We quickly finish our beers and head for the door. We're just walking away from the bar when I realise I'm cold.

"Shit, I forgot my jacket. I'll be right back," I call as I turn around.

"Hang on; I'll come back with you," Lily says as she grabs my arm, but I shake my head.

"It's fine. You two go on ahead and grab the drinks and find the guys. I'll get my jacket and use the restroom. I can see the bar from here; it's not like I can get lost," I laugh. Lily and Rachel share a look, but I start pushing them toward the other bar where we think the guys are. "Go, I'll be fine. I'm the big city girl, remember," I laugh, and they both nod and turn towards the other bar.

"Well, hurry up. I would hate to tell Luke I lost his first girlfriend in years," Lily chuckles as I shake my head at her and head back to the bar.

As soon as I walk in, I head straight for the booth we'd just been sitting in, which has already been taken up by a group of lads.

"Hey, any of you seen a jacket?" I ask as I reach them.

"Yeah, we just put it behind the bar, sorry," one of them replies.

"No worries, at least it's safe. Have a good night," I reply with a smile as I head towards the bar that already seems busier than before. I look around and realise I may be better off going to the restroom first and then waiting to get my jacket.

I walk to the back of the bar to the restrooms and see a small queue. I go to get my phone out to let the girls know I might be a while when I remember Rachel still has it. "Well, that was a good idea," I mutter to myself. By the time I finally enter the restroom, my bladder is close to bursting.

As I leave, I realise the queue has gone but the bar looks even busier. I step forward and get ready to push my way through the crowds when I feel something dig into my back, and a hand clamp over my mouth as I'm dragged backwards.

"If you scream or fight, you will find out what happens to uppity British bitches who are too big for their britches around here," someone growls into my ear as they pull me backwards, and I'm slammed into a wall. I look up and see Robert standing in front of me.

"I don't want any trouble, just let me go, and I won't shout or tell anyone," I say as calmly as possible, trying to hide that my heart is pounding in my ears.

"I don't think I'm ready for you to leave yet," Robert growls as he leans over me, pushing me harder against the wall.

Chapter Seventeen

LUKE

I race towards Rachel and Lily. It's now been fifteen minutes since they last saw Elli. They called me when they couldn't find her. Elli isn't the reckless type, nor would she want to worry the girls, which has me worried something *is* wrong.

As I reach them, I see Elli being helped out of the bar, visibly upset; my old friend Andy who owns it is with her.

I call her name as I rush towards her, the second she sees me, she runs straight into my arms. I can feel her shaking as she cries. The girls start asking her where she's been and if she's okay, but I hold her tight for a moment before taking her head in my hands and leaning back to look at her tear-soaked face. I see a swollen mark on her cheek like she's been hit. I look further down and see that her top is ripped on one shoulder. I quickly shrug off my jacket and put it around her shoulders.

"Who did this to you, baby?" I ask as I look into her bloodshot eyes.

"Robert, he tried to drag me into a storeroom, but I fought him and managed to get away," she whispers.

"I heard her scream when I was going to get some more bottles and found her by the toilets. Robert must have hidden away, but I know he's been watching her all night," Andy says as I look at him. I kiss Elli's head and look at Mitch and Billy, standing with the girls.

"Stay with her!" I growl as I walk out of Elli's arms and head straight to the bar, where I can see Robert looking through the window. I hear Elli shout my name but know the others will stop her from following me.

I storm into the bar and head straight for him. He turns around smirking.

"I wondered when you'd show up," he says as I see his hands curl into fists, but I'm quicker. I swing and hit him in the jaw, harder than I've ever hit anyone before.

"Get him outside, Johnson," Andy calls behind me. I grab hold of Robert's shirt and drag him to the door, where I throw him out of the bar and onto the street below.

"You think you can touch my woman and get away with it? Get up, you fucking prick!" I roar as I storm towards him. Robert jumps to his feet with his fists up.

"Your woman? All I saw was a fucking cock tease," he laughs at me as blood trickles from the side of his mouth. He turns and spits it out, but whilst he's distracted, I punch him again, which causes him to fall back into the road. I stand over him and am about to grab his top when I feel two sets of arms grab me from behind.

"Luke, enough, the sheriff's coming," Billy snaps as he stands in front of me with his hand on my chest. I look up as the sheriff jumps out of his car and straight towards us. Dan rushes up to him, and I know he's filling him in on what happened. Dan's an officer and will try to ensure I stay out of the shit. I shrug Mitch off me and look around to see

Elli standing in Rach's arms, watching me as she cries. I head back over to her, and she walks straight into my arms.

"I'm sorry, I'm here now," I whisper into her hair as she clings to my shirt.

"Elli, Luke, the sheriff needs to talk to you both."

I look up from Elli's head and see Dan looking at me.

"How much trouble is Luke in?" Elli asks as she looks at Dan.

"I'll know more when we get to the station," Dan says, looking at her with a soft smile. I put my arm around Elli's shoulder and lead her to the police cruiser Dan directs us to. The sheriff walks over and stops in front of us.

"We won't keep you any longer than we have to. Luke don't worry about what happened. Everyone saw Robert fall from the bar and hit his head on the way down. The bar staff asked you to remove him from the premises. So, no matter what's said, there are plenty of witnesses to back your story." I give the sheriff a nod and help Elli into the back seat before sitting next to her. I instantly pull her to my side and hold her as we head toward the station.

An hour and a half later, I've been interviewed and let off with a warning. I'm sitting outside the room Elli's being interviewed in when she walks out. She looks exhausted and like she's ready to drop. I stand up, and she walks to my side and leans into me as I wrap my arms around her.

"We'll be back in a minute, y'all," Dan says as he walks away from us. I sit down, pull Elli onto my lap, and hold her close.

"I want to go home, cowboy," she says quietly into my

chest. My heart breaks as I hold her closer. There was me thinking we could have some sort of life here, but now she wants nothing more than to get the hell out of Alabama and back to Chicago. She feels safer in the city than she does here with me.

"Okay, legs, I'll sort out tickets as soon as we get back," I whisper into her hair. Elli pulls away from me and frowns.

"What?"

"You said you want to go home," I answer, confused.

"I meant the ranch," she whispers. I look into her eyes and run a knuckle over her bruised cheek.

"I thought you might have been scared off after tonight," I admit. Elli shakes her head as she looks at me.

"He's one dickhead. It'll take more than him to scare me off from all of this," she says with a small smile. I lean in and kiss her lips gently.

"You have no idea how happy I am to hear you say that," I whisper as someone clears their throat in front of us.

"Y'all can head off. We don't need to know anymore tonight," Dan says as he looks at us. We stand up and shake his hand.

"Thanks for everything, Dan," I say as Elli steps out of my arms and hugs him.

"No thanks needed. Take your girl home, and both of you get some rest. Enjoy your Christmas," he says as he winks at me. We both say goodbye as Dan walks us to the station's front door, and I find Billy's truck parked outside.

"Dan hollered and said you would need a lift," he calls as he steps out of the truck. I thank him before helping Elli climb in. As soon as I'm sitting next to her, I pull her against me.

"Dan said he'll be facing more jail time after tonight," Billy says next to us. Elli nods.

"He's been charged with attempted kidnapping with intent to rape, or something like that," she says. I tighten my hold on her as I take a deep breath to control my temper. Elli places her hand on my knee to calm me. Despite everything she has been through, she still tries to help me. I turn my head and plant a kiss on her head.

"Rachel and Lily are both in the house; they're feeling guilty about what happened," Billy says next to us.

"Well, they shouldn't. It was my fault; I should never have gone off without them. They told me not to, but I didn't listen," Elli sighs as she leans against me again. I watch as she closes her eyes and her body quickly relaxes as she dozes off to sleep, exhausted after everything she's been through tonight.

"How did you end up with a girl like that?" Billy chuckles next to us.

"I have no idea how I got so lucky," I admit as I look down at her. "She fought Robert with everything she had," I whisper as I watch her sleep.

"Rachel says she'll never forget how she looked as she walked out of that bar," Billy quickly glances at me, and I can see the sorrow in his eyes. "I don't think any of us will," he adds. I take a deep breath and try not to remember how she shook in my arms.

"He'd seen us last night and wanted to get one over on me. She was just a pawn in his little game," I growl quietly.

"Well, he won't be messing with either of you again for a long time," Billy says as he turns on the long drive to the ranch.

As we pull up outside the house, I can see it's lit up and know Mom and Pops will be up, as well as the girls. I gently shake Elli's shoulder.

"Come on, legs. Let's get you inside," I whisper. Elli

nods, and I help her out of the pickup. I hold her against me, offering some support as we start walking towards the house. We all look up when the front door opens, and my little sister barrels toward us.

"Oh, Elli, are you okay?" she cries as she throws her arms around her, almost knocking her off her feet.

"Lily, I'm fine," Elli chuckles as she straightens up under my sister's weight. Lily steps back, and even in the dim porch light, I can see she's been crying. Elli looks at her and offers a soft smile. "Honestly, I'm fine, and if you say you're sorry one more time, I'll scream," she says before looking behind Lily at Rachel, who's standing on the porch looking out at us, hugging her shawl around her shoulders. "Same goes for you," Elli warns her with an arched brow. Rachel nods and offers her a small smile. I place my arm back around Elli and start leading her into the house. As soon as we are through the door, we're greeted by Mom and Pops, as I expected.

"Bless your heart Elli, your poor face. Do you need anything? Have you iced it?" Mom asks as she fusses over Elli and pulls her out of my arms, hugging her. Elli smiles at her as she nods her head.

"Dan gave me an ice pack in the station and some painkillers. I'm good for now. Luke may need some for his hand, though," she adds, winking at me. I look at my hand and realise it's still a little swollen, I've also split two knuckles.

"I hope you knocked the prick's teeth out," Pops says next to Mom. I look at him and feel my jaw clench.

"He better hope I never see him again," I growl as Pops nods in agreement. I feel someone pat my chest and look to see Elli smiling at me.

"Down boy, neither of us will see him again any time

soon. Does anyone mind if I go to bed? I'm exhausted," she says as she leans her head against me.

"Of course, you are. We'll see you tomorrow. Luke, don't get up to help in the morning. Spend time with Elli," Mom says before we say good night to everyone and make our way up to our room.

Chapter Eighteen

ELLI

I leave the bathroom as I dry my hair with a towel. As soon as we'd reached the room, I'd told Luke I wanted to get in the shower and wash the night away. I stood under the water scrubbing my skin until it ran cold. I just wanted to scrub the feeling of that bastard's hands from me.

I look up and find Luke lying on the couch, staring at the ceiling, with his hands behind his head.

"Okay, two things," I say, obviously breaking his train of thought as he turns to look at me. "Firstly, I think I may have just used a week's worth of water, and I need to apologise to your parents in the morning," I say as I walk around the bed and sit on the edge facing Luke, who chuckles as he looks at me.

"Secondly, what the hell do you think you are doing lying on there?" I ask. A small smile creeps across his face as his eyes soften.

"I wasn't sure if you would want me in your bed after everything you've been through tonight," he answers sheepishly. I shake my head as I climb into bed and move to my usual side before looking back at him.

"It's *your* bed; I'm just borrowing it," I reply with arched brows. Luke climbs onto the bed and lies next to me, smiling.

"It's *our* bed, and we are *sharing* it," he replies as he tucks some damp hair behind my ear. "How you feeling?" he asks softly as he cups my cheek. I open my mouth to answer, but he moves his finger over my lips. "Don't give me that 'I'm fine' bullshit. I know you better than that, legs," I look into his blue eyes and let out a deep breath.

"I was so scared, Luke. I had no idea if I would be able to fight him. He's so much bigger and stronger than me," I feel the tears slide down my cheek, and Luke pulls me into his arms, I lie with my head on his bare chest and try to stop myself from crying, but as soon as Luke runs a hand over my head, I finally relax and let down my guard.

"I'm sorry he put you through that. All because of some stupid argument we had when we were kids. He's never let it drop," Luke whispers as he continues to run his hand over my head and hold me.

"It's not your fault," I whisper as Luke kisses the top of my head again.

"I only promised you this morning that no harm would ever come to you, and then this evening, you were attacked." I pull away from him and look at him.

"How is that your fault? You didn't know what he was going to do. You didn't even know he was there last night. So no, it's not your fault, and I won't let you beat yourself up about it," I say as I wipe the tears from my face and look up at Luke from his chest. He looks down at me and wipes his knuckle across my bruised cheek, from where Robert had hit me in an attempt to silence me.

"I could kill him for what he did to you. No one will ever lay a finger on you again," Luke growls protectively. I move so my head is level with his.

"I believe you," I whisper as I press my lips to his. Luke kisses me back and rolls us to the side, so I'm lying on my back, and he's leaning over me. He pulls away from me too soon, and I frown at him.

"I swear to god, cowboy, if you give me any excuses tonight and leave me to relieve myself; I will take it you aren't interested," I warn. Luke looks at me wide-eyed for a moment before chuckling and kissing my nose.

"Well, that's me told," Luke laughs before leaning back over and kissing me lightly on the lips before whispering in my ear. "I knew you were in here last night playing with yourself. I stood in that shower imagining what you were doing as I stroked myself into the most intense orgasm I have ever had." I look up at him as I bite my bottom lip. Luke's eyes drift, stopping at my lips and back up again.

"Do you have any idea how sexy you look when you bite your lip like that?" he growls before taking my lip between his teeth and gently pulling it from mine. Luke runs his tongue over it, and I open my mouth to feel his tongue against mine.

"Baby, I want to kiss and taste every part of you. Are you going to lie there like a good girl and let me?" Luke whispers seductively into my ear before kissing my neck as his hands ride up my sides, pushing my t-shirt up. I feel his hands slide around to my back a little.

"Sit up for me," he demands; I obey instantly. "Arms up, baby," he adds before he slides his hands up my sides and arms, taking my t-shirt with them. Luke sits back on his heels and looks at me, taking a sharp breath.

"You're even more perfect than I dreamt you would be,"

he whispers before I reach up and kiss his lips, my hands tugging at the bottom of his t-shirt.

"If I'm topless, you should be too," I point out with a smile. Luke leans back and pulls off his top in one move. God, the muscles on this man should be illegal. I run my fingers across his smooth, broad chest and see it flex as he takes a slow intake of breath.

We're both topless, kneeling in the middle of the bed, staring into each other's eyes, when Luke threads his fingers into the damp hair at the top of my neck and grips it as his lips crash into mine, and we fall to the side. I just manage to stop myself from squealing from the shock. Luke looks down at me, smiling as he moves between my legs.

"Think you can be quiet enough so my parents don't hear us?" he whispers, chuckling at me.

"How many times have you said *that* in this bed?" I tease, smirking. Luke leans down and kisses my neck again; my eyes close as I moan quietly.

"I told you, I've never brought a girl home before. You are the first my parents have ever met," Luke says as his lips move from my neck across my collarbone and down between my breasts. He takes one nipple into his mouth and lets it slide between his teeth before releasing it with the slightest pop. He does the same with the other before kissing down my stomach. He looks up at me, and I see the softest look in his blue eyes.

"Lift your hips for me, baby." I do as he commands. His hands take the waistband of my shorts and pull them down, exposing me to him.

"I've dreamt about how this cute little pussy would look and taste," Luke whispers as he runs a finger between my swollen, slick sex and spreads me open for him. Luke nudges my legs; I smile as I place them over his shoulders. He looks up at me and grins wickedly.

"Don't choke me just yet, legs," he winks. Before I can respond, I feel his tongue flick across my clit, and all coherent thoughts are gone. Luke chuckles before he continues to lick, nibble and suck on my clit as he pushes one then two fingers into me.

All rational thought evaporates as the pleasure builds within me as Luke expertly coaches me towards the most intense orgasm I've ever had. All those months of teasing and winding each other up are finally undone as I grind myself against his face and fingers before becoming completely unravelled. I luckily have enough sense to grab a pillow and hold it over my face as I try my hardest not to scream as the pleasure crashes through me, leaving me shaking and gasping for breath.

I'm still breathless when Luke pulls the pillow from my face, and I see him grinning at me. I'm too incoherent to speak, so I grab his face and pull him down so I can kiss him. He chuckles against my lips as his bulge nudges me in just the right place; I'm still so sensitive that the slightest touch has me hurtling towards another orgasm.

"Tell me what you need, legs," Luke whispers as he pulls away from me slightly.

"All of you," I gasp as I reach down and feel his impressive length with my hand. This man feels so good naked.

Luke takes my wrists, moves my hands, so they are above my head, and holds them in place as he looks into my eyes.

"Wrap those gorgeous legs around me, baby." I do as he asks as I feel him slowly slide into me.

"Fuck!" I curse as I feel him filling me, stretching me in the most perfect way. I can hear him breathing deeply as he slowly eases into me. Luke stops moving, and I know he's completely in; he kisses me and holds still, letting me get used to how he fills me.

"Luke, please," I beg, the feeling of him and the pressure in the right spots quickly becoming too much. I rush towards another orgasm, but I need him to take me the rest of the way.

"I know, baby, I've got you," he whispers into my ear before moving again. I pull against his hand holding my wrists down, desperate to touch him, but he smirks at me.

"Hold still, or I'll be forced to get some rope and tie you up," he chuckles as he picks up speed and his thrusts become more forceful. With my legs still around him, we move in perfect sync, he quickly pushes each of my buttons, and I orgasm again. He holds me tight, so I'm moaning into his chest whilst biting his firm pec, trying desperately to be quiet.

"Fuck baby, you feel too good," Luke groans into my shoulder as he lets go of my hands, and I wrap them around his neck, threading my fingers into his hair and tugging slightly, which earns me a growl as he lifts his head to look at me, both of us slick with sweat, and gasping for breath as we move together. I can taste the salt from his sweat on his lips as I kiss him, and it turns me on further.

This man is taking me to highs I have never experienced as he whispers the dirtiest things in my ear.

"You feel so good, baby. You were made to take my cock. You're going to take it any way I give it to you. I will have you in positions you have only dreamt of, and each one will make you cum harder than the last."

"Fuck," I gasp, so close to another wave, not knowing where one ends and another begins.

"One more baby, and I'll be right there with you," he

growls against my lips as he grinds into me. Hitting my G-spot and clit with each thrust, sending me over the edge as I dig my nails into his back and bite down on his shoulder to silence my screams. Luke, however, isn't so quiet.

"Fuck, Elli!" he growls aloud as he thrusts into me three times, hard. I feel him cuming inside me, which only causes my orgasm to intensify.

We lie in each other's arms, gasping and shaking. I knew sex with Luke would probably be good, but that was something else.

"Told you we'd have fun with your legs wrapped around me," Luke whispers. I turn to look at him and burst out laughing, quickly slamming a hand over my mouth, remembering we are within earshot of his parents, sister and grandmother.

"A bit late, I think they heard us," he chuckles before leaning over and kissing me. "Remind me to take you far away from this house tomorrow so you can be as loud as you want," he whispers against my lips, causing me to grin at him.

"It wasn't me who was the loudest," I reply with a wink. Luke smirks before pressing a kiss to my lips again.

"What can I say? You have driven me mad, teasing me with those skirts and tight pants for six months. I may have lost control a little," he chuckles.

"Why do you think I wore those skirts and tight trousers?" I reply and quickly screech, laughing as Luke jumps over me and places himself back between my legs with a devious grin.

"Oh baby, you're such a tease. Let's see if we can be a little quieter this time," he whispers as he nudges me with his quickly growing cock.

"I doubt it," I reply as he slides into me again, and my eyes roll to the back of my head with pleasure.

Chapter Nineteen

LUKE

I wake up surprised by the sun shining brightly through the window. I never sleep past dawn. It's been programmed in me too long to wake up with the cockerel and get to work. I roll over and realise I'm alone. Elli's side of the bed is cold, so she's been up for a while. I look at my phone on the side and see it's nine in the morning.

I jump out of bed and throw on my sweatpants before rushing out of the door, worried that Elli has regrets over last night or that she's hurting after Robert's assault. Anger still tightens in my gut whenever I think about him having the audacity to lay a finger on my Elli. I'll destroy anyone who tries to hurt her again.

As I reach the stairs, I smell something I've never smelt before, followed by the sound of my niece and Elli giggling. I rush down and find them both in the kitchen. Elli and Skyla are standing to the side, rolling what looks like pastry and cutting it into rounds and stars. While Mom and Rachel sit at the table drinking out of mugs and laughing every time, Skyla tries to put more flour on the side, and Elli tries to stop her.

"Looks like sleeping beauty is finally awake," Rachel calls as she sees me. I flip her off quickly before Skyla sees; Elli looks at me and smiles. I plant a kiss on Mom's cheek as I pass her. As soon as I'm next to Elli, I take her chin and lift her head gently so I can see the bruising properly.

"It looks worse than it is," she says, smiling. I lean down and place a gentle kiss on it before kissing her on the lips.

"When I woke up, and you weren't there, I was worried you regretted last night," I admit into her ear quietly as I wrap an arm around her waist. Elli puts her arms over my shoulders and looks into my eyes as her smile lights up her whole face. She shakes her head, and I kiss her gently on the lips again. "Glad to hear it," I whisper, smiling before stepping back.

"How long have you been up?" I ask as I look around and see a big saucepan of some brown fruity mixture and some tarts on a cooling rack. I reach over to pick one up, but Elli slaps my hand away.

"Since seven. Don't touch those; they're fresh out of the oven. Here," she turns, picks one off a plate, and holds it up for me to take a bite. I tighten my arm around her waist and hold her close as I look down at the pie and see it's got a pastry star on the top. "Don't be a chicken and try it," Elli laughs. I take a cautious bite and slowly chew it. The insides are still warm, and I can taste the raisins and currants I saw her buy the other day. There is also a hint of cinnamon, nutmeg and brandy to it. I look into her eyes and blink.

"What the hell? That's amazing!" I blurt out as I take the rest from her hand and shove it in my mouth as she giggles.

"It's a mince pie. Told you they were great," she laughs as she wipes some crumbs from the side of my mouth.

"I don't know why Santa likes them. They're yucky," Skyla says as she scrunches up her nose. Everyone laughs as Elli leans around and wipes some flour off Skyla's cheek.

"I think they are more of a grown-up treat, hun," Elli says before quickly moving the flour out of Skyla's reach as she tries to put even more on the board. I laugh as I go to reach for another mince pie, but Elli knocks my hand away again.

"Stop it."

"But they're nice," I pout.

"Well, you can wait for the next batch. How about you make yourself useful and ladle some of that almost cooled mincemeat into the sterilised jars there."

"There's enough here to make a hundred pies," I exclaim, looking into the big stock pot. I hear Elli giggle next to me.

"Your mum wanted me to make her some for the store cupboard. If you're not going to help, go and have a shower or something. We'll be finished in here in about fifteen minutes," Elli says as she tries to push me away from the mince pies. I lean down to kiss her but use the distraction to quickly grab one and run out of the way of the dish towel she throws at me. I hear Mom and Rachel roar laughing as I rush past them, shoving the mince pie in my mouth.

"Uncle Luke, Santa's watching!" Skyla calls after me as Elli laughs. I head to our room and into the shower, feeling happier and more content than I have for a long time.

Chapter Twenty

LUKE

This has been the best Christmas Eve I've had for a long time. I spent the whole day with Elli and the family. We laughed until we cried; Elli and Skyla sang Christmas songs and made us watch the Muppet's Christmas Carol while we ate popcorn and drank eggnog. Elli wasn't a fan of the eggnog, and I couldn't help chuckling when she tried it and pulled the same face I suspect Skyla did when she tried the mince pie.

"I think they are more of a grown-up treat, hun," I mocked her, chuckling, before running from her and Skyla, who chased me out into the dining room and around the table until they cornered me and sprayed whipped cream at me. We ended up all covered in cream, and when I found Mom watching us, I expected her to say something. But thankfully, she was too busy laughing to tell us off.

Throughout the day, Elli has been sitting on the couch next to me or on the floor between my legs so she could sit with Skyla in front of the fire. Skyla has demanded Elli's attention continuously, and Elli's been happy to oblige. She even managed to persuade Skyla to put a mince pie on the plate for Santa with the Christmas cookie she had made with Mom and Rachel a few days ago. Watching Elli laugh and play with Skyla made me wonder what kind of Christmas Elli has had since her nan died.

Elli told me she was always looked after in the foster homes, but she always missed the traditions she had with her family. It couldn't have been easy for her to miss so much from such a young age. Today I made sure she had the chance to do some of those traditions again, and the smile it brought to her face lit up the whole damn house. There's no mistaking Elli's effect on this house and family. Everyone seems happier just by being in her presence. Or is it that I'm just happier and noticing everything else more?

It's now late in the evening and Elli and I are sitting outside on the love seat on the porch. Elli is curled up against my side with her legs over mine and a blanket over our laps as I hold her in my arms. Both with a hot chocolate, which I put a shot of bourbon in to keep us extra warm. Billy, Rachel and Skylar have gone to bed in their rooms here in the main house, the same as the rest of the family. Everyone wants to wake up in the same house in the morning to open the presents that have taken up the best part of the family room.

"I don't think I've ever thanked you," Elli whispers, dragging my thoughts back to now. I turn my head and frown at her.

"What for?" I ask as Elli looks up at me.

"For asking me to come with you and giving me the chance to enjoy Christmas again," she answers. "Especially as you never bring anyone home with you," she adds with a smile. I lean down and kiss her gently.

"You are special to me, legs; you always have been.

That's why it was so easy to bring you home. It felt right because you mean more to me than anyone else ever has," I tell her honestly. Elli smiles at me before kissing me back just as gently.

"You are special to me too," she whispers before leaning against me. I kiss the top of her head and tighten my arm around her. In only a few minutes, I feel her body weight shifting against my chest and look around to see her eyes closed and the mug of hot chocolate starting to slip out of her hand. I reach down, take the mug before it falls, and tuck the blanket around her tighter, not wanting to move her, as I'm enjoying holding her in my arms as I relax, listening to the sounds around us.

It doesn't take long until the temperature drops too low, and I know I should get Elli in before she gets cold. I consider waking her but opt to carry her instead. I stand up with her in my arms. She starts to stir, but I tell her to go back to sleep, and she does after placing her arms around my neck.

Slowly, trying not to wake her, I carry her through the house and up the stairs. Mom comes out of the bathroom and smiles at me as we get to the top.

"Get her to bed; the poor woman must be exhausted," she whispers before cupping my cheek. "Merry Christmas, Son."

"Merry Christmas, Mom," I whisper as she walks off towards her room, and I head to ours.

I walk in and carry Elli to the bed before placing her gently on top of the covers. I keep the lights off as I go to the en-suite to wash up. As I walk back into the bedroom, I find Elli standing up from the bed.

"Sorry, did I wake you, legs?" I ask quietly as I walk over

to her and place a kiss on her lips. Elli looks up at me and smiles.

"Your absence did," she replies. "How long have I been asleep?" she asks, looking around.

"Not long, only half an hour, if that," I answer as I run my finger over the bruising on her face. She rolls her eyes and takes my hand before kissing me on the lips whilst putting her arms around my neck.

"I'm going to wash and brush my teeth; you can stay here and be all sexy for when I come back," she winks before turning away from me. I grab her arm and pull her back to me as she giggles.

"Are you giving orders now, legs? What am I, just a piece of meat to you?" I ask with a grin on my face. Elli smiles as she nods.

"A hot piece of meat at that," she replies with a wink as she turns away from me again. This time I don't spin her back around. Instead, I wrap an arm around her waist and pull her back to me, so her back is against my front as I flatten my hand against her stomach.

"Maybe I don't want to wait for you to get washed; maybe this hot piece of meat wants you now," I whisper into her ear as I undo her jeans and slide my hand inside them until my fingers find her clit. Elli moans and lifts her arm and wraps it around my head so she can thread her fingers into my hair.

"We need to be quieter than last night; your sister was complaining this morning," Elli whispers before gasping as my fingers pick up speed.

"I know, that's why I came up earlier and fixed the headboard to the wall," I chuckle in her ear before nibbling on her earlobe. Elli gasps as she gets closer to her climax.

"And what about us?" she pants, right on edge now. I

turn us, so she's in front of the bed and pulls my hand from her jeans before quickly pulling them down to her ankles as she moans aloud for me not to stop. I place a hand on the centre of her back and bend her over in front of me before placing my hand between her legs so I can push my fingers into her, lowering my own pants. I lean over her so she can feel the tip of me against her, and I can whisper into her ear.

"You can scream into the covers, and I'll use your shoulder like you used mine last night," I whisper before biting her lightly on the shoulder. "I like that you left your mark on me; now I want to mark you and make sure everyone knows you are mine," I growl as I thrust into her and Elli gasps into the bed covers. I hold still for a moment before moving in and out of her as I reach around and play with her clit. In minutes she is orgasming around me as I continue to pound into her. I manage to coax two more orgasms from her before I realise I can't hold off any longer.

"Fuck baby, give me one more, cum for me, baby," I groan into her shoulder before burying my face into her neck as she comes apart at the seams. I release into her, her contractions milking every last drop out of me, and we fall onto the bed in a happy, sweaty heap.

Chapter Twenty-One

ELLI

I wake up to the feeling of Luke kissing me softly on the top of my head. I open my eyes and realise I'm lying on his bare chest, his arms tightening around me.

"Merry Christmas, legs," Luke whispers as I look up to find him smiling at me. I move and kiss him on the lips.

"Merry Christmas, cowboy," I whisper back as I move, leaning on his shoulder and looking into his eyes. Luke runs a finger over the bruising on my face before pressing a light kiss on my cheek. "It's fine, Luke, it doesn't bother me," I sigh as I see the anger in his eyes again.

"It bothers me," he sighs before smiling at me. "I could get used to this waking up with you," he adds as he rolls over and nudges his way between my legs, making me giggle.

"Is that so?" I ask, smiling up at him. Luke leans down and kisses my jaw.

"It has its uses," he whispers as his lips move down my neck.

"And what are those?" I ask, giving him better access to me whilst he positions his already hard cock at my entrance.

"Easy access for one," he whispers as he starts to enter me.

"Uncle Luke! Elli! Santa's been!"

I scream as Luke curses and looks wide-eyed over his shoulder to see Skyla standing in the doorway.

"Skyla! I told you not to go in!" Rachel yells as I hear her laugh before the door slams shut.

"Please tell me your niece did not just see what I think she saw!" I demand as I throw a pillow over my face.

"Uh yeah, I think she did," Luke mutters, looking behind him, "at least the blankets covered us. But remind me to put a lock on that door!" he states as he falls next to me, neither of us now in the mood to continue what we'd just begun.

"I think that's our cue to get up and see what Santa has brought us all," he says as he pulls the pillow from my face whilst smiling down at me.

"He's brought me a bundle of embarrassment, that's for sure," I groan as I look at him, trying not to laugh. I hear Billy roar with laughter and know Rachel's just told him what Skyla walked in on. I look at Luke; neither of us can hold it anymore, and both burst out laughing. Luke leans over and kisses me.

"Come on, legs. I'm sure you have been a good enough girl for presents," he winks before climbing out of bed.

"You got me a present?" I ask excitedly as I sit up, holding the duvet against my chest. Luke grins as he pulls up his sweatpants.

"You'll have to get your sexy backside downstairs and find out, won't you," he replies winking. I squeal excitedly as

I jump out of bed, quickly find my pyjamas and pull them on.

Less than five minutes later, Luke and I walk down the stairs, hand in hand, laughing until we see Billy standing in the hallway waiting for us with a grin on his face and his arms crossed over his chest.

"Hey Skyla, what did you say Uncle Luke was doing with Elli?" Billy calls out towards the lounge.

"Mama said they were hugging, Daddy! Stop being silly; I want to see what Santa brought me!" Skyla calls from the lounge as I hide in Luke's chest. I hear Luke and Billy both burst out laughing.

"At least you're finally getting some, brother," Billy roars as he walks away from us, and Luke leads me into the lounge, where the rest of the family are all sitting around grinning at us.

"Billy Johnson, you leave your brother and poor Elli alone, do you hear me," Luke's Grandma demands, winking at me as I sit next to her. Luke perches on the arm of the chair and places an arm around my shoulders, chuckling.

I look around at the Johnsons, all sitting together in pyjamas, a massive tree in the centre of the bay window surrounded by presents in all shapes and sizes. Everyone smiles and laughs as Skyla bounces on her grandad's knee excitedly. Looking at Luke's family, I realise how much I miss my own. I wish my nan and dad were still here to be a part of this. They would have loved Luke's family and felt at home on the ranch. I imagine Nan and Luke's Grams baking together in the kitchen, sharing recipes and stories. Dad would have been out with Luke and his Pops, working with the animals and helping them fix things; it was what he was good at.

But then again, if they hadn't died, would I ever have come to the States and met Luke for us to have experienced any of this? In short, no. I would never have left them, and they would have never come with me. Sometimes our pasts may cause us undeniable pain, but we must experience it to get to where we are destined to be. And right now, I feel like this is where I belong, surrounded by a wonderful family at Christmas, with someone who makes me feel cared for.

"You okay, legs?"

I turn to see Luke looking at me, the worry evident on his face. I smile as I nod my head.

"I sure am, cowboy," I reply as he leans down and kisses me softly on the lips.

"I'm glad to hear it," he whispers as he smiles.

"Luke, this one's for you."

We both turn to see Lily holding a present up, who reaches over and takes it from her. Luke looks at the label and opens the wrapping. Inside is a box; when Luke opens it, I see his eyes light up before he looks up at his brother, who's watching him.

"I noticed your tools were looking a little worse for wear and thought you might need them soon," Bill says as Luke smiles at him.

"Bro, these are perfect. Thank you." He looks at me and smiles. "They're wood carving tools. I've had the same set since I was ten, so they're a little worn."

"You carve wood?" I ask, surprised. Luke nods as he looks over my head at his sister, who holds a box towards me.

"This one's for you, Elli."

I take it from her and look at the label.

Elli,
Just a little something to remember a perfect day.
Yours
Luke xxx

I excitedly open the gift box and gasp when I see what's inside. I gently lift out a wooden figure of a woman on the back of a horse. I look up at Luke, amazed.

"You made this?" I ask as he nods.

"It's you and Mitzy; I thought that way you'll always have something to remember your first time riding a horse," Luke explains, smiling.

"Luke, it's beautiful," I whisper, taken back by how thoughtful his gift is. "I had no idea you were so talented," I add, smiling.

"Luke, this one's from Elli," Annie calls out. Luke reaches over and takes the gift bag from her. I'm suddenly very nervous about this gift. After him putting so much thought into mine, I should have done more. I watch nervously as he opens the gift box in the bag.

"A new hip flask," he exclaims excitedly as he turns and looks at me.

"I heard you moaning about Oliver losing yours about a month ago, so I ordered it. It's engraved," I explain, chewing on my lip. Luke turns the flask around and reads it.

Cowboy,
Now you have no excuse not to invite me for a drink,
Love,
Legs Xx

Luke looks at me with his mouth hanging open.

"When did you get this engraved?" he asks as I chew my lip nervously.

"When I ordered it a month ago," I admit quietly.

"But, we weren't," he starts and quickly stops, realising we aren't alone. I smile as I shake my head.

"I know; I took a risk. Thankfully, it paid off," I whisper as I look into his blue eyes. Luke grabs the back of my head and pulls me into a lip-crushing kiss.

"Oh, it paid off, legs," he chuckles as he leans his head against mine. "Thank you," he adds before kissing me once more. I'm just about to answer when someone screams in my ear as they jump on Luke and me.

"You're both amazing! Thank you! Thank you! Thank you!" Lily screeches until Luke finally gets her off me enough so I could look at her.

"What did you do?" he asks, laughing as his sister hugs him and me again.

"You said she wanted that purse, but you had already brought her the bag she originally asked for, so I got it for her," I laugh as Lily jumps away from me and shows off her new Ralph Lauren handbag and purse to Rachel and her mum.

"I can't believe you got that for me! You didn't even know me!" Lily says excitedly, but I shrug.

"I'm not going to lie; I wouldn't have without the 50% discount I get there."

Lily stops dead and stares at me straight-faced.

"You get half off everything?" she asks with her mouth hanging open. I nod, chuckling.

"I won the ad campaign four months ago, and Ralph loved it so much I get 50% off for life," I answer with a shrug. Lily looks from me to her brother before addressing him.

"If you don't marry her, I will!" she shouts as we all burst out laughing. "What? I'm serious!" she declares, looking around.

"I'm just glad you like it, Lily." I laugh as I lean against Luke's side. We sit together, watching everyone exchange gifts. Annie and William like the wine glass set Luke insisted we get them between us; Lily tends to steal their wine glasses and not bring them back. Billy and Rachel loved the hamper I had put together from Luke and me, filled with Billy's favourite drinks and Rachel's favourite wine and toiletries. Luke was amazed when he realised I had also picked out a bottle of his favourite bourbon to fill his new hip flask, which he did almost instantly.

"Elli, there's one left here for you," William calls as he passes Lily a box for me. I frown as I look at it and read the label.

Legs,
Happy Christmas.
Love,
your favourite cowboy Xxx

I look up at Luke, who is smirking next to me. I open the box and screech happily as I pull out my gift.

"You got me my own hat!" I laugh as I look up at Luke. He takes the white cowboy hat from my hands and places it on my head.

"I'll make a cowgirl out of you yet," he replies, chuckling, as I look up at him grinning.

"You just want to keep your hat when she's been drinking," Billy laughs from across the room where he's sitting with his daughter on his lap and his wife by his side.

"That's another reason I got her it," Luke laughs as I slap his arm playfully.

The rest of the day is spent laughing and joking; I sit with Skyla and play with her new doll house her Uncle Luke has been helping her Daddy build. She loves the dolls I had gotten for her to go with the house.

I've also spent time laughing in the kitchen as I help Annie and Rachel to prepare the great feast they put on. It's not much different from what I used to eat in the UK. They had mashed potatoes instead of roasties, but I know some people do that in the UK too. One thing that was missing was the Yorkshire Puddings! They've never heard of them before, and I've promised to make them the next time I'm there for a visit.

It's been the most magical day, and by the end of it, I'm exhausted, full and happy.

We're all winding down late in the evening with a glass of bourbon when Skyla comes running in from the dining room, screeching.

"Daddy, it's snowing!" she yells, trying to drag her dad from the couch where he's curled up with Rachel.

"Sweetie, it never snows in Alabama," he says, half asleep.

"It is! Look!" she yells as she rushes for the window. Lily sits up from where she's lying to look and jumps to her feet.

"It *is* snowing!" she yells as she and Skyla rush out of the room. We all jump to our feet and race for the front door, pulling on our boots as we all try to get out at once.

As we gather on the porch, we see the lightest snow dusting on the floor and flakes falling from the sky. I feel two arms wrap around me from behind and smile as I lean back into Luke as he holds me tight.

"I can't remember the last time I saw snow here," he says as he rests his head on my shoulder.

"Not since we were kids," Billy says next to us, where he has an arm around his wife.

"The perfect end to the perfect Christmas," Luke whispers into my ear before kissing my cheek. I can't help but smile, I couldn't agree more.

Chapter Twenty-Two

LUKE

I wake up with Elli curled up against me. The sun is just starting to creep over the horizon, and for a moment I consider staying in bed and just holding her. But today's our last day on the ranch, and there are a few things I need to do. I want to get them done fast so Elli and I can have lunch by the lake before a family farewell dinner tonight.

I kiss the top of her head and slowly pull my arm out from underneath her. Elli moans slightly in her sleep but doesn't wake up. I quietly grab my jeans, t-shirt and flannel from the wardrobe before sneaking into the en-suite to dress.

As soon as I'm finished, I write a quick note to Elli, telling her I'll be back for her at eleven and have her jacket, boots and hat ready.

I sneak down the stairs and find Pops in the kitchen.

"Wasn't expecting you this morning," he says as he pours some coffee into a mug and hands it to me.

"There are a few things I need to get sorted before lunch. Is Billy meeting you in the usual place?" I ask as I take a sip of my coffee. Pops nods as we both turn and walk to the back door where our boots are waiting for us. We pull them on quickly and head out to the stables, where we find Billy yawning whilst feeding the horses.

"Thought you would be sleeping in after last night. I was sure you'd get lucky," Billy laughs as I approach. I punch him on the arm playfully.

"Pack it in, Billy," Pops sighs as he frowns, "I've never seen your brother as happy and carefree as he is now," Pop adds as he turns to me and smiles.

"Hate to agree with the old man, but he's right. Never seen you smile or laugh as much as you have this week," Billy chuckles. "You and Elli seem good for each other," he adds as he runs a hand over Mitzy's side. I lean on the fence and smile at them both.

"She makes me happier than I ever thought possible," I admit as I look at them. "It's taken us a long time to finally get to where we are, and I don't plan on messing it up now that we're here."

"You think she's the one?" Billy asks as I take a sip of my coffee; I look at him and smile.

"I know it. No one else on this earth could make me as happy as she does. I'll marry that woman someday," I admit grinning at my dad and brother, who are both grinning back at me.

"And the big plan? Where does that sit with the two of you?" Pops asks as he looks at me, and we smile at each other.

"That's actually why I'm out here with you both. I'm going to need your help."

Elli

I've been awake for a while and am sitting in the kitchen, having toast with Rachel and Annie. Skyla is back in the family room playing with her new doll house, and we can hear her talking away to herself. That little girl has stolen my heart; the whole family has. To think I was as worried as I was to meet them, and now I can't imagine them not being in my life.

"I can't believe you're both going back tomorrow already. It feels like you've only been here a few days," Rachel moans. I take a sip of my coffee and nod.

"I know. I wish we didn't have to go back," I sigh.

"Well, you're welcome to come back at any time, even if you leave Luke in the city," Annie says, smiling at me.

"You might want to take that back; I'll be here every weekend," I joke. "Anyway, Luke might not want to bring me back," I try to make a joke of it, but by the look Annie gives me, I know I failed.

"Are you kidding? That man is besotted with you," Rachel exclaims before turning it to Annie.

"I can hand on heart say that I've never seen my baby child as happy and content as he's been this week. You two have something extraordinary," Annie adds as she reaches over, takes my hand, and squeezes it. "I can see how much you care for him," she says with a motherly smile. I look at her nodding. "Then I can't see any reason why the two of you won't be back regularly," Annie adds, winking at me.

"You could always move here and start a new life on the ranch?" Rachel suggests grinning. I can't help laughing.

"Now that sounds like an idea I could get behind," I declare with a smile. I look up at the clock and realise it's almost eleven. I tell Rachel and Annie I'm meeting Luke and head out the door as I pull on my boots. I get to the stables five minutes early; eager to see Luke as I've missed him all morning.

"Hey, El's!"

I turn to see Billy walking toward me. "Hey, you seen Luke?" I ask as he approaches.

"He just messaged asking me to saddle Mitzy up. He's running late after Pops asked him to sort something," Billy says as he waves me towards the stables. As I walk in, I hear my phone beep in my pocket.

Luke: Hey legs, I'm running late, sorry. Any chance you remember the way to the lake? I'll meet you there. Xxx

Elli: Yeah, I do. I'll leave here in a minute once Mitzy is ready. Need me to bring anything? Xxx

Luke: Only yourself. See you in a bit. Be careful. Xxx

I roll my eyes and put my phone back in my pocket.

"She's all ready for you. Don't know how long Luke will be, though," Billy calls as he walks Mitzy over to me.

"I'm meeting him by the lake. Can you give me a boost up, please?" I ask. Billy smiles at me and nods before helping me to climb onto the big horse. I thank him before heading off toward the lake.

Thankfully, I have a good sense of direction and don't get lost. I'm there within fifteen minutes. Mitzy and I may have gotten a little carried away and picked the speed up to a gallop for part of the way. I never thought I would get to ride a horse, let alone love it as much as I do. It feels natural, like it was something I've done my whole life, not five days.

We slow down as we come to the trees that separate the lake area from the rest of the ranch and make our way through them. As we clear them, I see Luke shaking hands with a guy who gets into his truck and drives off.

"Who was that?" I ask as I trot up to Luke, who frowns at me as he jogs up to us and takes Mitzy's reins.

"Did you run here?" he asks as he helps me down from the saddle. I shrug my shoulders before answering.

"A little," I admit, giggling at the shocked expression on Luke's face.

"You have no fear of that horse, do you?" he chuckles as he kisses me.

"What can I say? I love her," I answer with a grin. Luke puts his arm around my shoulder and guides me towards a blanket on the ground that I hadn't noticed before. "What's all this?" I ask as I look down and see food and a few beer bottles.

"I wanted our last afternoon here to be perfect," Luke says as he sits on the blanket and pulls me down so I'm sitting between his legs. He wraps his arms around me and holds me tight as I lean against him.

"Everything about this week has been perfect," I answer as I sit back and close my eyes, listening to the sounds of nature around us and just feeling content whilst wrapped in Luke's warm embrace.

"I don't understand how you could choose the city over this," I sigh as I run my fingers over Luke's arms which are still around me. "What made you leave?" I ask.

"It was a mixture of things. I felt like my life was set out from the moment I was born. Like everything was decided for me, I was going to stay on the ranch, and that was final. I wanted more. I thought the city would give me that and make me happier," Luke says as he looks out over the water.

"Well, from what I've seen this week, you're much happier here than in the city," I point out. Luke makes a noise as if to agree before running a finger over my arm.

"What about you? You told me the other night that you moved to the States to find a place that could be home. Did you find it in the city?" He says softly as he draws lazy circles on my hand as I lean my cheek against his.

"No, the city isn't home. This feels more like home than anywhere I've lived since my nan died," I admit.

"Would you move here?" Luke asks. I turn my head so I can smile at him.

"Maybe," I chuckle before going back to leaning against him. "Being here with you has made me feel things I never thought I would feel again," I admit. Luke lifts my hand and threads our fingers together.

"I spent my whole life on this ranch, but it has never felt more like home than it has this week here with you," he says as he looks down at our joined hands. "So, what happens when we return to the city?" he asks quietly. I turn my head so that I can look at him.

"What do you mean?" I ask cautiously, worried this has all been part of the act.

"I mean, what happens with us? I know we started by pretending…"

"Are you still pretending?" I ask, interrupting him as I spin around and stare; his eyes bulge from his head as his jaw drops.

"Hell no! I don't think I ever was, don't ever think any of this week has been an act, because it wasn't, not for a moment!" Luke says as he takes my face in his hands and kisses my lips before looking me in the eye. "I can't go back to the way we were, baby. Now that I have you, I don't plan on ever letting you go. I want to stake my claim on you and make you mine. No man can ever touch, or taste you again."

"That's good, because I don't want any other man. I want you, cowboy," I reply with a smile before turning back around so I can sit with my back against his chest again. "Let's go back and just take each day as it comes," I say as I lean my head back against his shoulder.

"Sounds good to me, legs," Luke replies as he kisses my cheek.

"You never said who that man was before," I point out.

"He's a lawyer. Pops is getting rid of this land, and that's the one dealing with all the legal crap that goes with it," Luke says. I turn back around to look at him.

"He's selling? Why?" I demand.

"He doesn't use it, and it's just here," Luke replies with a smile.

"But what about your dream of building a house here?" I ask, but Luke takes my face in his hands and kisses me softly.

"I'm sure I will get my dream house one day; I already have my dream girl," he says with a grin before knocking me onto my back and lying over me as I giggle underneath him. Luke nudges my legs with his, and I open them for him. He leans down and looks into my eyes with the softest smile on his face.

"I love you, Elli; I have for so long. Now I have you; I don't want anything to fuck this up for us," he says as he brushes some of my hair from my face.

"I love you too. I have a feeling we are going to be just fine," I reply as he leans down and kisses me.

Chapter Twenty-Three

LUKE

I park my car and head into Elli's apartment building. We've been back from Alabama for a week, and I've been here every night since. I've only been going to my place to get a change of clothes or use the gym and never staying away for longer than a couple of hours.

Whilst we were on the ranch, we didn't get any work done, so we've been working flat out since. Today was the big day, and we presented our work to the clients and our bosses. We won it, like I knew we would.

We had managed to keep our relationship a secret until this afternoon when we were told we had won the campaign. I'd just been so happy for us that I'd scooped her off her feet and kissed her straight on the lips in front of the whole company. Everyone had been waiting for us to get together anyway; even Anthony wasn't surprised.

I let myself into Elli's building using the keys she gave me, and I say 'howdy' to the doorman on the way to the elevator. He gives me a quick wave as I hurry on up.

I've just been to my building to use the gym and get

some clean clothes for work tomorrow. Elli has persuaded me to lose the tie. She's right; there's no point not being the real me when I'm here. I know I wanted to find out who I am away from the ranch, but there's no need to be uncomfortable at the same time.

I get off the elevator on Elli's floor and head straight for her apartment. It's a lot smaller than mine, but it's closer to work, so more accessible for us to go back and forth to the office to get what we need whilst working during the holidays. I open her door and close it behind me.

"Legs, I'm back! I have everything to make you the best steak you've ever eaten. Plus a few treats," I call out as I hang my jacket on the hooks by the door and kick off my shoes. I look around when Elli doesn't respond. I place my bag of clothes on the floor and the shopping bag on the side in the kitchen and look around, frowning.

"Legs, where are you?" I call as I head to the back, where her bedroom and bathroom are. I hear the shower running as soon as I get to the doors. I open my mouth to call through to her when I hear her sobbing. I rush into the bathroom and see her sitting on her shower floor, crying into her knees. I reach up and feel the water is running cold; she must have been there for a while. I turn the shower off and grab her towel.

"Come on, baby. Let's get you out of there," I whisper as I help her to stand up. I look at her face and can tell she's been crying for a while. Elli wipes her face and takes the towel from me. I watch as she wraps it around herself before taking another to wrap her hair. As soon as she's done, I pull her into my arms and hold her for a moment, then lead her into her room and get her to sit on the bed.

"Hey, talk to me, legs. What's happened?" I ask as I kneel before her and cup her cheek with my hand.

"I've just been going through the emails I ignored whilst we worked on the presentation, and I've had one from the landlord. They're putting the rent up. I can't afford it, even with the pay rise. I will have to find somewhere else, but I can't get the money together for a deposit; all my savings went into moving here," she sobs. "It feels like every time things are going right, something is always waiting to knock me back down."

I pull her into my arms as she starts to cry again.

"You know there's an easy solution, don't you?" I whisper into her ear as I kiss her cheek.

"What?" Elli sniffs.

"Move in with me," I suggest. Elli looks up at me.

"What?"

"You heard, move in with me," I repeat as I smile at her.

"We've only been together two weeks. What will people think?" Elli asks, frowning at me.

"How many people do we care about?" I ask as I raise one eyebrow. Elli smiles slightly then.

"Just your family," she says quietly. I feel my smile getting more prominent as hers does.

"Do you think they will say anything if we move in together?" I ask as Elli shakes her head.

"Okay," she says as she looks at me, smiling as fresh tears fill her eyes.

"Okay? You going to move in with me?" I ask, grinning. Elli laughs and nods before I pull her into my arms and kiss her.

"You are the best thing that ever happened to me," I whisper into her ear before kissing her neck, and she melts into my arms.

Epilogue

ELLI

It's been six months since Luke took me to Alabama for the first time. We've since moved in together and been back twice. Once for Robert's trial, where he was sentenced to three years. The second was for Skyla's sixth birthday. She now calls me Auntie Elli and will soon become a big sister, Rachel is five months pregnant.

Everything has been perfect between us, and I can't imagine life without Luke and his family in it. We speak to his parents a few times a week, and I now call them Mum and Pops. Lily and Rachel message me almost daily. Lily has started her own photography business, and I've been helping her with website design and advertising her work worldwide.

As perfect as things have been, the last few months have been challenging as Luke was asked to help the company open new branches, which has meant he's away as much as he's been home, but he calls me every single morning and night, and we make up for the lost time when he's back. He's currently away again and won't be back until tomorrow. I've been in a foul mood all week because of it, I'm miserable when he's not here, but I try not to show it, as I know he would hate to know I was upset.

"Howdy, Legs!"

I jump from my seat and turn around to see Luke standing by the lift, holding a bouquet of flowers.

"Oh my god!" I scream rushing to him. He catches me as I jump up and wrap my arms and legs around him.

"Easy, legs. Anyone would think you missed me," Luke chuckles as he holds me. I grab his face and kiss him on the lips.

"What are you doing back so early?"

Luke lowers me onto my feet. He looks down at me and smiles.

"Got an early flight. Hope you're not busy as we have a plane to catch in an hour," he answers, pulling two tickets from his back pocket. I grab the tickets and look at them.

"Are you serious?" I ask.

"Yep, Billy's already left my pickup at the airport. I've cleared it all with Anthony, and I've been home and packed your stuff," he says, grinning. I squeal and throw my arms around his neck.

"You're the best cowboy ever!" I laugh, kissing him. Luke chuckles as he tucks a stray section of hair behind my ear.

"I figured I owed you after being away so much recently," he says, smiling at me sweetly.

"This is a great way to make up for it," I reply, kissing him again.

Five hours later, we pull up to the main house. I jump out of the truck and rush inside, desperate to see Mum and Pops, only to find it empty. I walk back to the front door, sulking. I look at my phone and see I still haven't had replies from Rachel and Lily. I messaged them on the way to the airport, but there has been nothing in reply.

"Where is everyone?" I ask. Luke looks around and shrugs.

"Must be out on the land or in town. What do you fancy doing while we wait for them?" he asks, bringing our suit-case to the front door. I look at him and grin.

"Can we go and see if we can still get to the lake? We didn't have time last time we were here," I ask.

"You just want to ride, Mitzy," Luke laughs as I nod eagerly.

"It's a bonus," I chuckle. Luke takes my hand, and I squeal whilst rushing to the stables. My favourite horse is in the paddock, who rushes over to greet me.

"Hey girl, I've missed you," I coo over her. Luke takes my hand, and we go to the stables and get Mitzy and Reggie ready.

In fifteen minutes, we are on the outskirts of the woods that lead to the lake.

"It looks like it's a clear path," I say as Luke jumps down from his horse and walks up to mine. He helps me down, and we take their reins.

"Let's go by foot just to be on the safe side," Luke says as he takes my hand before we walk through the trees.

As soon as we walk into the clearing around the lake, my heart jumps to my throat.

"Oh, it looks like someone had the same idea as you. Look at that house," I gasp as we walk a little closer. I barely register Luke letting go of my hand and taking Mitzy's reins. I'm so mesmerised by the building and surrounding areas ahead of me.

There, not far from the water's edge, is a house, about the same size as Billy and Rachel's, with a porch and a stable and paddock next to it. There is now a dirt road that leads away from the house to what I'm guessing is the main road. I look around further and see a fire ring with logs for seats around it.

"They put the fire ring exactly where you wanted one," I point out to Luke as I turn to face him.

"That's because I put it there," he replies smiling at me. I freeze as he walks up to me and takes my hands.

"That solicitor wasn't here about someone buying the land; he was here about Pops signing it over to me to build our new home. We're both happier here than in the city, and we speak about moving here constantly, so I took a leap of faith and built the house. Well, Pops, Billy and I built it; I did all the furniture and patched up the bits Billy messed up," he explains, grinning at me. "I also made sure there was a paddock and stables. I bought Reggie and Mitzy from Pops because I know how much you love her," he adds.

"When?" I ask, looking around, amazed.

"I haven't been travelling for work; I've been working from my laptop. I've been coming home to get this ready for you, for us," Luke says as he cups my face with his hand.

"I don't want to stay in the city, and neither do you. You say daily that you would rather be here, so I organised everything. Let me know when you want to move, and I'll sort it out. You can continue working for Anthony, or you can start up your own advertising business, and web designing for the local businesses like you said you would like to."

"We can really move here?" I ask, scared to believe it's true. Luke nods, smiling.

"Yes, legs. We can really move here. But I would like there to be one condition to it," I look at him and frown, but he grins at me as he drops down to one knee. I gasp as I stare at him with a hand over my mouth.

"I love you, Elli, more than I ever thought it possible to love anyone. You make me the happiest I have ever been. Please say you will move here with me, not as my girlfriend but as my wife. Say you will marry me." I stare at Luke there on his knee and grin.

"I have one condition," I reply, smiling playfully. Luke looks up at me, grinning.

"And what's that, legs?"

"That we can be married and settled here within the next seven to eight months," I answer, chuckling as Luke's face goes from confused to shocked in seconds.

"Are you?" Luke asks, as his voice breaks.

I nod as I pull the pregnancy test from my pocket, where it's been hiding since we got off the plane.

"I'm pregnant," I reply as the tears start rolling. Luke jumps to his feet and picks me up before spinning me around as we laugh. I hear a scream coming from the house. I see Lily and the rest of our family and friends piling out, shouting and cheering. I turn back to Luke as they all race towards us and smile.

"You name it, and you can have it, legs. Whatever you want, it's yours," Luke declares as he places me on my feet. I put my arms around his neck and look up into his tear-filled blue eyes.

"Between you, the house and baby, I could never ask for more," I reply as Luke kisses me, and my heart flutters as I realise, I'm finally home.

Next in the Lakeside Ranch series

vinci-books.com/dancingwithdan

She wanted independence. He vowed to protect her. Love was the risk neither of them planned on.

Lily Johnson escapes to a quiet Alabama cottage for freedom—but danger follows. When fear sets in, she turns to her brother's best friend, Officer Dan Watkins. As sparks fly, secrets stir. Can their forbidden love survive the fallout?

Turn the page for a free preview…

Dancing with Dan: Chapter One

LILY

"What's the matter? You look like you haven't slept in a month."

I turn to look at my new sister-in-law, Elli, and sigh.

"I feel like it. Every goddamn morning, Pops, Luke and Billy wake me up, talking outside of my window. I get they have to be up at the crack of dawn to work, but I don't!"

"Trust me, I get it; Luke is far from quiet in the mornings," Elli smiles sympathetically as she picks up her mug and frowns at it before taking a sip. "I miss real coffee as much as you are missing your sleep," she sighs, leaning back into her chair and placing a hand on her swollen belly.

At seven months pregnant, she looks ready to pop. Her bump is much bigger than Rachel's was in either of her pregnancies.

"No one can miss anything as much as you miss real coffee," I laugh, sitting at the kitchen table opposite her.

"Yeah, it might be my fault that Luke is waking you up. He's working more with each passing day. He says it's so he won't feel bad for not helping out as much when the baby arrives. But personally, I think he's avoiding spending time with my moody ass."

I laugh as she takes another sip of her drink, turns her nose up and places the cup back on the table.

"They could at least make this stuff taste like real coffee," she groans, pushing the mug away as if it offends her.

I absolutely love this woman. The best thing to come out of her and my brother's relationship is that I have the big sister I always wanted. Don't get me wrong; my other brother's wife, Rachel, is also a hoot, and I love her unconditionally. But with Elli, we have this connection and love of all the same things. She is also closer to my age, which I guess helps.

When she and Luke moved to the other side of the ranch four months ago, I couldn't have been happier to have them so close. I get to spend nearly every day with my favourite person. Even if she's now pregnant and can't come on any nights out, the fact she's close is enough.

"Legs? Why are you here and not resting back home?"

I turn to see Luke walking into the kitchen, closely followed by Pops and Billy. He heads straight to Elli and kisses her whilst placing a hand on her belly. The two of them will make the best parents to their tiny human when they're born.

"I told you I'd planned on coming over today to help Lil update her website," she replies, smiling, before it slips from her face. "Talking of Lil, you guys need to stop waking her up by being loud outside her window every morning!" she warns Luke before looking behind him to where Pops and Billy are both standing. They all instantly start protesting that they are quiet, but I roll my eyes whilst shaking my head.

"You are far from quiet, and you know it."

"Lily, if we were that loud, Grams would be complaining as well," Billy points out.

"Grams is nearly a hundred and as deaf as a fence post. She would sleep through the end of the world!" I shake my head again, knowing they won't listen.

I thought that with Rachel having Skyla and baby Imogen, I would no longer be seen as the baby of the family, and I would be taken seriously now and again, but I guess not.

"Thanks for trying, Elli. But we all know they won't pay a damn bit of notice to me or anything to do with me. Not until I finally move out anyway." I stand from my seat and walk over to place my mug in the kitchen sink.

"You are too young to move out, young lady, and you know it," Pops says, standing before me with his arms crossed.

"Luke was twenty when he moved out and went to university. Billy moved out at twenty-two; why am I any different?" I protest as I face my dad with my arms crossed over my chest.

"Because it was different with them. They can look after themselves."

"Why because they are male? Just because I was born female does not mean I'm incapable of living on my own or standing on my own two feet, Pops." I throw my hands up as I turn and walk out of the kitchen.

"Where are you going?" Pops calls after me.

"To get some more pictures for work! If that's okay with you? Or do I need a chaperone? Since I'm too weak and helpless to do anything alone."

I don't bother waiting for a reply or listening to whatever is being said in the kitchen. I grab my camera bag from the pegs at the front door and pull on my boots, not stopping until I am outside to tie them.

I drop to the porch floor and lace my walking boots, trying desperately to push away the irritation causing every muscle in my body to tense. I'm tired of being the baby and being treated differently from my brothers. So what if I'm a girl? It doesn't make me any different from them. I know Pops is just old-fashioned, it's his generation, and he doesn't mean anything by it, but it doesn't stop it from sucking, nevertheless.

"You know their heart is in the right place."

I turn to see Ma walking out of the front door behind me.

"You are his baby, and he worries about you; we all do," she says softly as she sits beside me on the porch.

"I'm not the baby anymore; he has grandkids now," I point out, which earns me a raised brow.

"But they aren't *his* babies. Not in the same way as you are," she reaches over and tucks some hair behind my ear.

Ma will always be the one to defend Pops and my brothers when they upset me; I know she's doing it to keep the peace, but sometimes I wish she would take my side, but she never does. The only one who ever seems to have my back is Elli, but even then, she doesn't like to cause arguments or for something to drive a wedge between her and Luke. They have only been married for a few months and are still very much in the honeymoon period.

I stand from my spot on the porch and pick up my camera bag. I need some space to calm down and recharge my tolerance levels.

"I gotta go. See you later, Ma." I turn my back to her and walk towards my car. Eager to place as much distance between myself and this house as possible. I hear Ma shouting for me to be careful, and I wave my hand in acknowledgement, not bothering to turn or reply.

I climb into the car and pull away from the house more aggressively than planned. The tyres skid momentarily on the gravel before getting traction and guiding me onto the ranch's driveway.

As I head to my favourite woods, I think about moving out of the ranch. If I did, I wouldn't need to answer to my family as much because right now, I have to tell them where I'm going and who I will be with. Even at twenty-two years of age, they treat me like a teenager.

Unlike my brothers, I've never been in any trouble with the law, and let's face it, they'd find out as the sheriff's deputy is Luke's best friend, who tells him everything that's been going on in town. Or there's the gossip tree that Ma is part of. I swear if someone sneezes in the wrong direction, the house phone rings with someone telling her about it.

I pull off our drive and onto the main road that passes several other ranches and leads to Mitchan Woods. By the time I reach my usual parking spot, I've decided that when I get home, I will start looking into the housing market and find somewhere to buy or rent. I need to be independent, which won't happen while I live under my parent's roof.

Dancing with Dan: Chapter Two

DAN

I walk out into the mild afternoon sun and shield my eyes from the glare coming off the police cruiser in front of me.

"Keep your door closed and locked, ma'am, and I'm sure you will have no more problems," I say, turning to look at old Mrs Hall.

"I have lived in this house all my life, and I ain't ever had to lock my door before," she argues. I roll my eyes as I turn my back to her and head towards the car.

"Things change, Mrs Hall. This old town isn't as it used to be. You have a good day now, and call if you have any more problems," I add before climbing into the car, where Sheriff Hobbs is grinning at me like the child he is.

"You fucking prick."

Sheriff Hobbs roars, laughing as I pull my seatbelt around myself.

"Mrs Hall was robbed, Deputy Thomas. It's your duty to protect our community and investigate the crime," he states, trying desperately to keep a straight face.

"She left her back door wide open, and an animal got in

and ate the sausages she left out on the counter. That's not a crime, it's stupidity!"

Sheriff Hobbs roars, laughing again as he drives us slowly through town. He starts listing the things we need to get sorted out, but I'm not paying attention. I'm nodding and humming in the right places, but inside I'm screaming for him to shut up and let me out of this goddamn car.

We pull up outside of the station and climb out with the Sheriff still talking away about fuck knows what.

"I'm fixin' for a salad. I'll be right back," I call, jogging away from him and the station. I hear him shouting for me to pick up his usual. I hold up my thumb without turning to check he can see me.

As soon as I'm out of view, I tone the jog down to a slow walk and shove my hands into my trouser pockets.

What the hell am I doing with my life? Being a police officer is all I've ever wanted to do. But, nothing exciting ever happens in this small town. I know all officers feel like this eventually, which is why the retirement age is relatively young compared to other forces in the US or even just here in Alabama. But in our town, the biggest crime is the occasional bar brawl, a drunk and disorderly, or even an animal stealing sausages from an open window or kitchen door. Where's the excitement in that?

I've been feeling more and more trapped recently like nothing is ever going to change in my life. It could be because I've watched my best friend, Luke, fall in love, get married, and now have a baby on the way in the short space of twelve months. It could also be because I can't seem to meet anyone who keeps me interested for more than a few days. I've dated or slept with near enough every woman in this tiny town, and I still haven't met anyone I want to share things with, like late-night rides or drinks in town with friends. Maybe I've been a player for so long that I don't recognise a catch when I see one, or I've already missed my chance of happiness.

I stop outside the local café where we all get our lunches and let out a sigh before walking inside.

"Howdy, Dan!"

I turn to see my other best friend, Mitch, sitting at a table with his father. They work together, building barns and sheds for those in the community. They enjoy working together, and neither complain about anything other than the weather when it stops them from working. What I wouldn't give to enjoy my work as much as they do.

"Hey. How's it going?" I ask, heading over to the table and taking a seat. Mitch, Luke, and I have been best friends for as long as I can remember. Our families see each other as family, and we never have to worry about interrupting family time.

"Not much, just about to head over yonder to Johnson's place. His boys need a hand with a shed, and their pops isn't up for it like he used to be. He's starting to feel his age," Mitch's old man, Doug, chuckles as he drinks his mug of tea.

"You're both as old as dirt, old man, so pack it in," Mitch sighs, shaking his head at his father, who laughs at him before turning his attention to me. "You still hosting the game tonight? Need me to bring anything along?" Mitch asks.

"Nah, I have everything in. What time you coming over?"

"About seven?" Mitch asks.

"Yeah, sounds good to me. I'll let Andy know and see if he can make it," I reply, pulling my phone out of my pocket.

"I'll give Luke and Billy a heads up when I get to their place"

I nod as I read a message from a girl I saw last week. I roll my eyes as she asks what I'm up to and if I want to meet up. Isn't the fact that I haven't made contact with her in a week not enough of a sign that I'm not interested? She was loud and seriously thought too much of herself. She screamed high maintenance, which I'm not into.

Under the message, I see one I have been waiting for. As I read it, my stomach tightens with anticipation.

"Earth to Dan, you listening?"

I look back to Mitch and see him frowning at me.

"Sorry, what?"

"I said, who has pissed you off? You've been tense since you walked through the door."

I sigh, rub my tired face, and close my phone quickly, hoping he doesn't see the message.

"Just been a crap day. I got to go; Sheriff will wonder where his sub is." I stand up and say a quick "See ya later" to Doug and Mitch before heading over to the counter and ordering our food.

I can feel Mitch's eyes on me the whole time I'm there. He knows me better than anyone, even Luke, and will know something's going on. But how do I tell my best friend that I've been looking into moving out of state, and it may be happening sooner than I thought?

Dancing with Dan: Chapter Three

LILY

I'm so glad I came out today. The fresh winter air and the crunch of the leaves under my feet is just what I needed to clear my mind.

Now that I've calmed down, I realise I may have blown the whole situation out of proportion back home. I know Pops and my brothers don't mean any harm in how protective they are, but I feel smothered. I know it's time that I moved out and started living my life the way I want and not how others expect me to.

I have plenty of money coming in, so I can afford it. Thanks to Elli and all the work she has put into my website and helping me advertise, my photography sells worldwide, and I can't get the prints out quickly enough.

When I told my family I wanted to turn my hobby into a business, they were all encouraging and supportive, but I don't think they expected me to succeed. To be honest, I didn't expect to have the success that I did. In fact, I thought I would have to work a second job on top of this to make ends meet. Instead, I'm making four figures a month easily and even on a bad month, I never drop more than a couple of grand. That's more than enough for me to move out and live comfortably. Worse case I could see if any of my friends want to move in with me and share the bills. Anything has to be better than still living at home when you are nearly twenty-three years old.

I stop in my tracks as I spot a doe a short distance from me. I squat down as slowly and quietly as possible whilst lifting my camera to snap a picture. Just as I'm about to take one, a tiny fawn bounds into view and stands next to their mother. It's rare for a fawn to be born this late in the year, but it does happen. I know I can't miss the opportunity to photograph a fawn with the winter foliage around it. A picture like this could sell well.

I watch through my camera lens as the mother feeds and tries to keep the fawn under control. She is fighting a losing battle as this one seems to be full of beans and unable to stay still for longer than a few seconds at a time.

I follow them from a distance for about half an hour, unable to resist the cuteness of the fawn as it leaps around its mother and begs for attention. I have more than enough pictures to work with, but I can't seem to stop. I love nothing more than watching wildlife as it goes about its day, none the wiser that they are being watched. These two creatures in front of me are beautiful and mesmerising.

Just as I snap a picture of the doe reaching up to pull some foliage from a bush, something catches her attention and mine. I watch her ears start moving around, and she looks towards her right as if expecting danger. The fawn picks up on this and quickly moves to her side, and they also start looking around, mimicking their mother's behaviour. I look to the side of them and spot it: a cougar hiding in the bushes. It's so fixated on its prey that it hasn't noticed me.

Luckily, Pops taught me from a young age never to go anywhere without a whistle to blow if I got into trouble or saw a creature I wanted to scare away. I lift the whistle to my lips and start blowing hard whilst jumping out of my hiding spot. I know it's a risky move; the cougar could attack me, but all I can think about is protecting the mother and her baby.

All three animals jump as the whistle blows for the first time. For a fleeting second, they turn to look at me, and I don't wait to blow it a second time, which successfully scares them away from me and each other.

I keep blowing the whistle repeatedly to ensure all creatures have left and are a good distance from me. The last thing I need right now is the cougar circling back around and coming after me. I don't want to be its replacement meal, thank you very much.

"Hello? Is anyone hurt out here?"

I spin around to where the voice is coming from the left of me. I stop blowing the whistle as they call out again, checking if I'm okay. I take a few steps towards the voice when a young man comes into view.

"Are you okay, ma'am? I heard your whistle."

"Yeah, sorry, I saw a cougar," I explain, waving the whistle at him. His jaw drops, and he starts looking around frantically.

"A cougar? Where?" He looks ready to run, and I can't help laughing.

"It's gone that way, I scared it off. You're safe, for now at least," I tease as I stop in front of him, and he visibly relaxes. "Lily Johnson," I announce, holding out my hand. He takes it in a firm grip and shakes.

"Tim Gerald."

"So what brings you out here, Tim?" I ask as I admire

his suit and tie. You don't look like you're hiking, that's for sure."

He looks down at his outfit and laughs.

"No, I'm taking pictures of a property my dad is trying to sell," he explains, rubbing his neck.

"Oh, you're Mr Geralds's son! The estate agent in town," I exclaim. What are the odds that I'm considering buying a place to live, and an estate agent walks right into my path?

"There's a cabin for sale around here?" I ask excitedly. Tim nods with a smile on his face.

"Would you like to see it?" he asks, holding out his hand and showing me the way. I quickly let him lead me out of the trees and towards a log cabin surrounded by nothing but trees, with a dirt road leading away from the property.

I couldn't even guess how many times I've been in these woods over the years. They've always been my favourite place to come when the guys were picking on me, or Ma and Pops were getting on my nerves, but not once have I ever seen this place. Sure, the woods are vast compared to the others around here, but to miss the cabin entirely is madness.

Tim starts telling me about the property as he leads me inside, and I look around.

The place is beautiful and rustic. Even with the thick dust that coats every surface, it looks perfect for me. There are two bedrooms, a large sitting room, and an open log fire surrounded by a beautifully carved fireplace. My brother Luke may be able to build just about anything with wood, and his carvings are always breathtaking. But there is something about this fireplace that even he couldn't achieve.

I walk up the wooden staircase towards the two rooms and bathroom. Again, everything is covered in thick dust and needs a good airing. The musty smell in the air would soon disappear if the windows were left open for a bit and the place had a good clean.

"How long has it been empty?" I ask as I look at the built-in wardrobe in the main bedroom. There is also a king-size wooden bed. I dread to think what lives in its mattress now; it would no doubt need a new one.

"Approximately three years. The structure itself is sound and needs very little work done to it, but the furniture inside and the plumbing may need to be torn out at new put in," Tim explains as he runs his finger over the top of a chest of drawers, leaving a long void in the thick dust.

"How much is it selling for?" I ask, looking out the window at the view of the forest surrounding the cabin.

"Why? You thinking of buying?" I can hear the disbelief in Tim's voice.

"Funny enough, I was going to come down and speak to your Pops later about any property he had for sale." I look around the main bedroom and can see myself at home here. "This would be perfect," I add with a smile.

Tim watches me for a moment before a big smile appears on his face, and he stands to attention.

"Tell you what, let me be the one to sell it to you, and we can come to an affordable deal." He steps forward and holds his hand out for me. "I promise I will look after you," he smiles. I take his hand excitedly and shake it.

"Deal."

Dancing with Dan: Chapter Four

LILY

A few hours later, I take a deep breath before walking into the house. I can hear from outside that the whole family is here, and I can't decide whether that's a good thing or not.

"Aunty Lily!" I only just catch an excited Skyla as she launches herself at me as soon as I enter the dining room.

"Howdy, Skyla. How was school?" I ask as I place her back on her feet. She may only be six, but she is too big for me to carry these days. I don't have the strongest arms, which is why I'm no good about the ranch. Even docile Mitzy, Elli's horse, can pull me if she wants something out of her reach.

"It was boring. They only let us paint for ten minutes. Instead, I had to do math," she declares as she screws up her face in distaste. I copy her, which earns me a smile.

"Only weirdos like math," I tell her.

"Uncle Luke likes maths, and you can't get much weirder than him," Elli laughs as she walks into the room carrying two plates. Okay, walk may be the wrong word; waddling may be more accurate for what she's doing.

"Legs, I told you not to carry anything," Luke declares, jumping to his feet to take the plates from her. Elli moves them out of his way and proceeds to place them on the table.

"Cowboy, I swear to God, I'm going to snap if you don't stop fussing over me like an old mother hen!" she warns with her hands on her hips. "If Rachel can carry Skyla whilst pregnant, I sure as hell can carry a couple of plates. Now sit down and shut up!" She points to his place with such force I have to bite my lip from laughing out loud when he does as he's told.

"By the way, it's math, not maths. You ain't in England now; there's no 's'at the end." Luke ducks quickly and scrambles out of Elli's reach as she goes to slap him around the back of the head. The rest of us roar, laughing as Luke laughs and pulls a pouting Elli towards him, making sure to keep her arms by her side as he kisses her.

"You are lucky there are children present, Cowboy," Elli warns, fighting back a smile. Luke leans in and kisses her again before letting her go.

"Right, stop winding up the pregnant lady. Sit down and eat," Ma announces as she walks into the room with two more serving dishes. Everyone quickly takes their seats around the table.

I say a quick 'hi' to Rachel as I sit beside her and press a kiss to Imogen's head as she feeds from her mother's breast. She is such a beautiful and content baby, the complete opposite of Skyla when she was born. Since the moment she found her voice, Skyla has made sure she always has everyone's attention. We were a little worried about how she would be when the baby was born, but she loves her sister more than anything in the world. She tells her stories, helps Rachel change her diapers, and gets her anything she needs.

"You alright, Lily?"

I turn to see Pops sitting at the head of the table next to me. He reaches over and places a hand over mine on the table.

"About what I said before," he starts, but I place my other hand over his and give him a smile.

"It's fine, Pops. There's no need for apologies," I reply. He nods once, and I release his hand so he can start piling the food on his plate.

I look around the table and start to dish up my own food. I love Ma's cooking, especially when she has made my favourites: fried chicken, mashed potatoes, and gravy. I place it on my plate, and soon, we all start digging in and chatting among ourselves. I make it halfway through my food before Elli gets my attention.

"Did you manage to get any good shots today, Lil?"

I look up from my plate to see her smiling at me. Nerves start to knot in my stomach as I nod slowly.

"Yeah, I saw a deer with a fawn," I explain. After a few minutes of the others asking about how old I thought the fawn was and wondering why it was born so late, Pops pipes in with another question.

"What else did you do today? You were out for a long time."

I chew on the inside of my cheek and take a deep breath.

"Well, I kinda bought a house."

I hear people's cutlery hitting their plates as Pop's mouth drops open.

"What do you mean you *kinda* bought a house?" Billy asks as I try to appear calmer than I'm feeling.

"Okay, I bought a house. A cabin in Michan Woods, to be precise. It's been empty for a few years and is a bit of a fixer-upper, but I fell in love with it as soon as I saw it and knew I had to own it."

Pop looks up at Ma, who is staring at me.

"Annie, have a word with your daughter," Pop warns as he points his fork at me.

"I don't need a word. I'm able to make my own decisions," I snap as I look at Pops.

"Lily, how did you afford to buy a house? Where will you get the money for the mortgage, repairs, furniture, and so on? I know you think you can afford this, but - "

I snap my attention to my mom, who's looking a little shell-shocked.

"I have plenty of money to do all of that. The cabin was a steal, and even Mr Gerald said it was a bargain. He's already put me in touch with a few people to help with the repairs, and they are coming out tomorrow to give me quotes."

"Nope, not happening. You are not moving out."

I turn my attention back to Pops, whose jaw is clenched as he shakes his head.

"You can't stop me from moving out," I point out, trying desperately to keep calm.

"Oh, just watch me, young lady. While you live under my roof, you will do as I say," Pop snaps, taking me by surprise. He never snaps at me, not like this anyway.

"That's the point, Pops. I won't be living under your roof," I say, standing from the table and looking around at my family. The girls all look like they don't know what to say or do, and the guys are tense.

"Lily, you are not moving into a cabin in the middle of nowhere. It's not safe," Luke starts, throwing his napkin onto his plate.

"Luke's right, I won't let you put yourself in danger like this," Billy adds as he pushes his chair back from the table.

"Oh, come on. You," I snap, pointing at Billy, "moved out when you were twenty-one. And you," I turn my attention to Luke, "went to university when you were twenty. What is the difference between you two and me?" I yell.

"Oh, don't start all this again. This has nothing to do with you being a girl. It's about you living in a cabin in the middle of nowhere!" Billy yells, causing Imogen to scream and Skyla to cry. Rachel stands from the table and looks at her husband.

"Stay and discuss this like adults. I will take the kids out." She starts to lead the kids from the room. But before leaving, she turns and looks at me.

"I will always have your back, but I agree with your brother. The cabin doesn't sound safe. If you want to move out, I will help you find a place myself, but please reconsider."

I watch as she leaves the room with the two crying kids.

"Now look what you've done. You upset the kids," Billy starts, but I turn to face him with a look that makes him stop in his tracks.

"You upset the kids. You were the one shouting like an idiot. God, you are all being so unreasonable." I turn to walk out of the door and hear Elli calling my name.

"Lily, stop, please. You know they are just worried about you. Come back and talk about this."

I turn around and see her standing up, leaning on the table.

"There's nothing to talk about. I'm moving out as soon as the cabin is ready. I'll leave sooner if you don't stop trying to control me and everything in my life!" I hear their raised voices as I walk from the room and up to my room.

I don't know why I thought they might actually support me in this. Let's face it: they will always see me as the baby of the family, no matter how old I am.

Dancing with Dan: Chapter Five

DAN

"And she thinks she's going to be just fine and dandy living out there in the middle of bumfuck nowhere. I bet she can't even get a phone signal out there!"

I look to Luke, who's been in a foul mood since he arrived. Billy hasn't been much better, but as always, Luke is the one ranting and raving, and Billy nods in agreement.

"I'm sure she has thought about all of that, Luke. Lily isn't stupid."

From the way the Johnson brothers glare at me, I know I've said the wrong thing.

"How would you feel if it was your kid sister? I bet you would be just as concerned," Billy points out as he shuffles the cards.

"The difference is my kid sister, and yours are two completely different people. My sister was knocked up by the time she was sixteen. Your sister studied hard and worked even harder to make a name for herself. Lily is level-headed; Sharon is not."

Billy mutters something under his breath as he starts dealing out the cards. I look to Mitch who is looking at us around the table, keeping his head down, whilst drinking my good bourbon. Nothing new there, then.

"Look, I get you are both annoyed as hell, shit, I get it. But moaning about it isn't going to change her mind. The paperwork's been signed, and she has the keys. There is nothing you can do about it." I pick up my cards and curse silently at my rubbish hand.

"Maybe," Luke mutters as he looks at his own cards.

"What do you know about the place? Any idea why it's been empty for years?" Billy asks. I shake my head whilst picking up my drink.

"Nothing about it rings a bell, but I'll have to ask about it at work."

"Well, if it's bad, you need to tell us. It might be enough to put her off moving in there," Luke says, sipping his drink.

"I'll see what I can find, but I'm not making any promises." I watch the two brothers nod in agreement. "Great, now can we please play a few rounds of cards before one of you gets called away by your ball and chains," I tease as Mitch laughs out loud. We love giving them both shit for being married. We know we can get away with it as their wives are great and like to wind them up as much as we do. The two brothers mutter something in agreement, and the game finally starts to unfold as their mood starts to lift.

It doesn't take long, and the conversation drifts to Billy's kids and Luke's baby on the way. The more they talk about them, the more jealous I become. I want what they have, and I'm once again reminded that I won't get that here, not in this town or maybe even this state.

It's half passed ten, and the brothers have left to get home to their families, leaving Mitch, me, and a bottle of bourbon. As usual, Mitch has drunk far too much to even think of attempting the short walk home so will crash in my spare room.

"You've been quiet tonight."

I turn to look at Mitch and find him watching me.

"I've not had much to add to the conversation," I answer, sipping my drink. I can feel Mitch still watching me and sigh as I look back to the sofa he is lying on. "What?"

"It was more than that. What are you hiding?"

"Nothing." I know I answer too quickly, and he picks up on it.

"How long have we been friends?" he asks, sitting up and placing his glass on the coffee table in front of him.

"Too fucking long," I sigh, downing the rest of my drink as I gear myself up for the long lecture I'm about to get.

"You are my brother, and I know when something's wrong. I saw how you looked at your phone in the café earlier, so spill it. What's going on?" Mitch is giving me his full attention, and I know I have no choice but to come clean.

"Fine, I'm sick of the job and regret becoming a police officer. Nothing ever happens around here, and I'm tired of the same old callouts. I feel more like animal control than I do an officer of the law." I wait for Mitch to say he told me so. He always said I was living a fool's dream when I went into the police. He thought I should learn a trade like him and that I would regret not listening to him. He never said anything again. Mitch isn't like that; he will sit on something, and when you prove him right, he will remind you he knows us better than we know ourselves and move on.

"You don't regret it, not deep down."

I stare at him for a moment before frowning.

"What? No big *I told you so*?"

Mitch shakes his head and runs his fingers through his hair.

"No, because I was wrong back then."

"Can I have that in writing?" I ask, amazed. He rolls his eyes and sits back on the sofa before putting his feet up on the coffee table and relaxing.

"You love your job, and you make a damn good cop. I might have had my doubts when you first said you wanted to be an officer, but you proved me wrong." He places an arm over the back of the sofa and relaxes a little further. "What you don't like is that it's not the fast life you imagined. You thought it would get you every girl in town, and for a while, it did. But now you want more and are worried you can't get it. The job is something you can control, so you choose to focus on that and want to change it when what you really need to do is stop sleeping around and settle down."

Damn, that's deep for him and also spot on, but I'm not going to admit that to him, and he knows it.

"Fine, don't accept that's the truth. But I saw the way you looked when the guys were talking about their kids. You want that, and there's no hiding it." Mitch pushes himself up from the sofa and stretches. "I'm going to crash; I have to be out of here by seven. Thanks for hosting the game and the drink. It's my turn next." He walks towards the lounge door before calling out, "Think about what I said, Dan. Ideally, before you end up old and alone because you have fucked every woman in town who will give you the time of day."

As Mitch disappears out of view, I sigh and sit back in my chair, wishing I still had some drink left in my glass. I know he's right, and I know I need to change something before I drive myself mad, which is why I've been putting things into place and will tell him when I am good and ready, whenever that may be.

Dancing with Dan: Chapter Six

LILY

I look around at the lounge and still can't believe it's mine. Everything in here belongs to me, and I couldn't be happier.

It's been a week since I first saw the property, and the excitement hasn't worn off. In fact, I would say I'm happier than I was that first day.

"Hey, Lil, are you in here?"

I turn to see Tim standing at the door with a smile on his face. He is dressed in his usual suit, shirt and tie.

"Hey! What are you doing here?" I ask as I head to the door and give him a hug.

Tim has been a fantastic help over the last week. He found me a plumber and electrician who both gave me affordable quotes. He's also been a great friend when I have needed one. My family is still giving me a hard time about this place, but Tim has listened as I moaned and gave me advice when I needed it.

"I thought I would pop around and see how the renovations were coming along." He looks around at the lounge where I have been giving it a fresh coat of paint. "It's looking so good in here; do you need a hand?" he asks, walking further into the room.

"You're in your suit," I point out, laughing. Tim looks down at his clothes and smiles.

"That's easily amended." He shrugs off his jacket and loses his tie. As he starts rolling up his shirt sleeves, I notice he has a full sleeve of tattoos on his right arm. He is also very well-built and obviously works out regularly.

"Like what you see?"

I look at Tim's face and smile.

"Sick tat."

He looks down at the tattoo and grins.

"Yeah, I love it. Pa makes me cover it when I'm at work. He says it's off-putting to the clients." He holds out his arm to give me a better look. I take his arm and start moving it around so I can see all the details.

"It's very cool. I love that flower; it's so pretty," I smile, pointing to a pink and white flower that twists and wraps its way up his arm.

"Not as pretty as you."

I slowly look up to find Tim smiling at me fondly. Shit.

"Uh, thanks." I let go of his arm and step back nervously. I see his smile falter slightly, making me feel guilty. "That's nice of you to say," I add, forcing a smile, hoping he thinks I'm just embarrassed and not uncomfortable. Tim smiles and takes a step forward.

"Lily, I was wondering - "

"Knock, knock! Anybody in here?"

I look to the door to see my brother's best friend, Dan, in his uniform smiling at me.

"What are you doing here?" I ask, rushing towards him, glad to put some distance between Tim and me. I throw my arms around Dan's neck, taking him by surprise. "Thank God you're here," I whisper into his ear as I let him go and hold his arm.

"Dan, this is Tim, who helped me buy the cabin," I announce, clinging to his arm. "Tim, this is Deputy Daniel Thomas," I add. Tim steps forward with his hand out.

"Of course, I know, Deputy Thomas. It's good to see you, sir."

Dan nods and shakes his hand.

"You're Tim Gerald, right? How's your father after the break in the other week?" Dan asks, causing Tim's smile to falter for half a second.

"He's fine. Luckily, very little was taken."

"You had a break-in? You never mentioned that."

Tim looks at me and smiles.

"Nothing to tell. Some morons came in and stole some petty cash. Luckily, Pa had cashed up that night, which he doesn't usually do." I can hear the frustration in his voice, and I have a feeling he is still pissed with whoever broke into his dad's place.

"Anyway, I didn't know you two knew each other," Tim points out, looking between Dan and me. I freeze for a second, wondering if Dan will let slip we aren't close, but instead, he places a hand over mine, resting on his arm and smiles down at me.

"We go way back, don't we, Lily bear?" the bastard smirks, using the stupid nickname he gave me when I was six. He knows I hate it, and there's nothing I can do about it.

"Sure do, Daniel," I reply, knowing he hates being called his full name as much as I do Lily bear.

"Well, I hope I didn't interrupt anything when I walked

in?" Dan asks, turning his attention to Tim, who steps back while shaking his head.

"No sir, I was just going to help Lily with some painting, but." Tim lifts his wrist and looks at his watch. I hear Dan snigger slightly and quickly try to cover it with a cough. I nudge him with my elbow whilst giving him a warning look. "Oh, I forgot I have a meeting in half an hour with Pa and a potential client, so I had better be off," Tim continues whilst grabbing his things and heading for the door.

"Thanks for popping around, Tim, and for all your help," I call out. He waves as he rushes out of the door.

"Take care, and shout if you need anything else done for the place," he calls back as he reaches his car.

"Thanks for all you've done for my Lily. I'll make sure to tell your father what a great job you're doing when I see him next," Dan calls out as he pulls his arm from me and wraps it around my shoulder.

"You are loving this," I growl through gritted teeth to ensure I still have a smile on my face.

"Every second," Dan replies, laughing. Tim pulls away too quickly, kicking gravel up from the makeshift road as he goes. As soon as he's out of sight, I shrug off Dan's arm as he laughs aloud.

"Aww, I think you hurt his feelings," he teases as he follows me into the cabin.

"I never thought I would be so glad to see you, jackass," I sigh as I fall onto the couch, which throws up a load of dust, causing me to cough.

"Nice place," Dan chuckles over the sound of my hoarse coughs.

"If you came here to wind me up, just leave," I snap before looking at him properly. "Why are you here? Did Luke send you?" I ask, crossing my arms over my chest. I watch Dan look around for somewhere to sit before wiping down a stool I've used to stand on when painting.

"Actually, Mrs Guest, who is your closest neighbour, by the way, has been noticing someone hanging around in the woods. She wanted me to check it out, and I thought I would give you a heads-up as well."

I guess that makes sense. Mrs Guest lives just over half a mile away, so whoever she saw could have headed this way.

"Thanks, I'll keep an eye out," I answer, standing from my seat.

"The place is nice. I can see why you like it. It's peaceful and quiet."

I look at Dan and frown.

"But?" I ask, waiting for him to agree with Luke.

"But nothing," he replies, standing from his seat and walking forward. "I get it, Lils; your family smoother you. They may only do it because they care, but they have to let you make your own decisions at some point. Let's face it, you're a damn sight smarter than my Sharon. As much as I love my nephew, and she is a fantastic mama, I do wish she had experienced more of life before having a baby."

"I wish you would tell my brothers that," I sigh, looking around at my lounge. I had hoped they would help me get it ready to live in. I wanted them to put the Johnson mark on the place—not because it would be done for free, but because it would be them.

"I have, and it didn't go down well. But I will keep trying, okay?"

I look at Dan and nod.

"Thank you, Daniel," I grin playfully.

Dan rolls his eyes and turns away from me.

"You're welcome, Lily bear," he calls as he walks towards the door. He stops as he goes to exit and turns back to look at me. "If you need anything and don't want to call your family, call me." He turns back around and pulls his business card from his wallet. "Any time, day or night, you ring me."

"I will. Thanks again, Dan," I say, taking the card.

"Any time, Lils. Be careful out here, okay? Keep your doors locked until I determine if this guy is dangerous to others."

I nod, not knowing what else to say.

Dan smiles and walks out of the cabin and towards the police cruiser.

"See you later, and try not to get eaten out here. The paperwork's a bastard for animal killings!" he yells as he climbs into the police car.

"Whatever!" I call back, laughing. I can see Dan grinning as he pulls away and heads down towards the road leading to town.

Walking back into the cabin, I close the door, look at it briefly, and quickly lock it. Even if my family think otherwise, I'm not an idiot. Dan said to be careful, and so I am.

I look around the lounge and sigh at the amount of work left to do. I might as well crack on and see how much I can get done before returning to the ranch. I pick up the paintbrush, hit play on my MP3 speakers, and start to paint as Taylor Swift's voice fills the room.

Elli's Nan's Mince Pies Recipe

Mincemeat

150g Currents
150g Sultanas
100g Raisins
75g Mixed peel
1 Lemon (zested and juiced)
75g suet (veg or meat)
1 Small cooking apple (peeled, cored and finely diced)
1 ½ tsp Mixed spice
1 tsp Ground cinnamon
200g Dark muscovado sugar
100ml Brandy

1. Put all ingredients, except the brandy, in a large saucepan. Cook over a low heat for 10 mins, stirring occasionally, until the sugar and suet have completely dissolved.

2. Remove from the heat and leave to cool to room temperature before stirring in the brandy. The mincemeat may look loose at this stage, but it will continue to thicken once cooled.

*Alternatively, you can purchase the mincemeat ready-made in jars where available.

Pastry

225g Cold butter, diced
350g Plain flour
100g Golden caster sugar

1. Rub the butter into the flour, then mix in caster sugar.
2. Combine the pastry into a ball – don't add liquid.
3. Use immediately or chill in the fridge for later

Instructions

1. Heat oven to 220C/200C fan/gas 7.
2. Roll out the pastry to 3mm thick.
3. Using a round cutter (about 10cm), cut out 16 bases and place them into muffin trays. Put 1½ tbsp mincemeat mixture into each.
4. Brush the edge of each pie with a little beaten egg.

5. Re-roll out the pastry to cut out stars and place them on top of the mincemeat.
6. Glaze with the beaten egg, and sprinkle with the extra caster sugar.
7. Bake the mince pies for 15-20 mins until golden brown. Leave to cool before releasing them from the muffin trays and dusting with a little more icing sugar before serving.

About the Author

D.E. Bartley lives in Wales, UK, with her husband, three feral boys, four cats, and a budgie.

To say her home is a madhouse would be an understatement, but she wouldn't have it any other way.

When she isn't running around after her tribe or driving her husband up the wall, she can be found reading and hoarding books like a dragon.

Nothing is as important to her as time with her family, and she loves her trips home to Cornwall with them more than anything in the world. What could possibly compare to sitting on a Cornish beach, with a glass of Cornish gin in one hand and an authentic Cornish pasty in the other, while the monsters, I mean children, play and bodyboard in the sea?

Absolutely nothing.

Acknowledgments

This was the first time I had worked with other authors to put together a selection of amazing stories, and I am so glad I joined this group, "A Homecooked Christmas". Each and every author has been so supportive and encouraging and made me feel like I belong. I was nervous going into the collaboration as I haven't been in the writing community for long, but I know I have made some really good friends and learnt so much from their experiences and advice.

As always, I couldn't have done this without the love and support of my husband and children. They are forever encouraging me to continue writing and are my biggest supporters. I love you all to the moon and back and always will.

Thank you to my fantastic friend Karen, who helped me with the US terms and sayings. Having someone to help this Brit write a US-based story really helped, as there are so many things we do here that they never do in the States. Karen, you have been such a support in all I do, and I couldn't thank you more.

Of course, I have to thank my other friends and family for pushing me to step out of my comfort zone and write whatever comes to mind. You are all amazing, and I love you all.

Most importantly, thank you to each of my readers who have encouraged me to continue this amazing journey. You guys really are the reason I do this, so thank you from the bottom of my heart.

www.ingramcontent.com/pod-product-compliance
Lightning Source LLC
La Vergne TN
LVHW041108190826
845923LV00037B/615

* 9 7 8 1 0 3 6 7 3 3 8 5 8 *